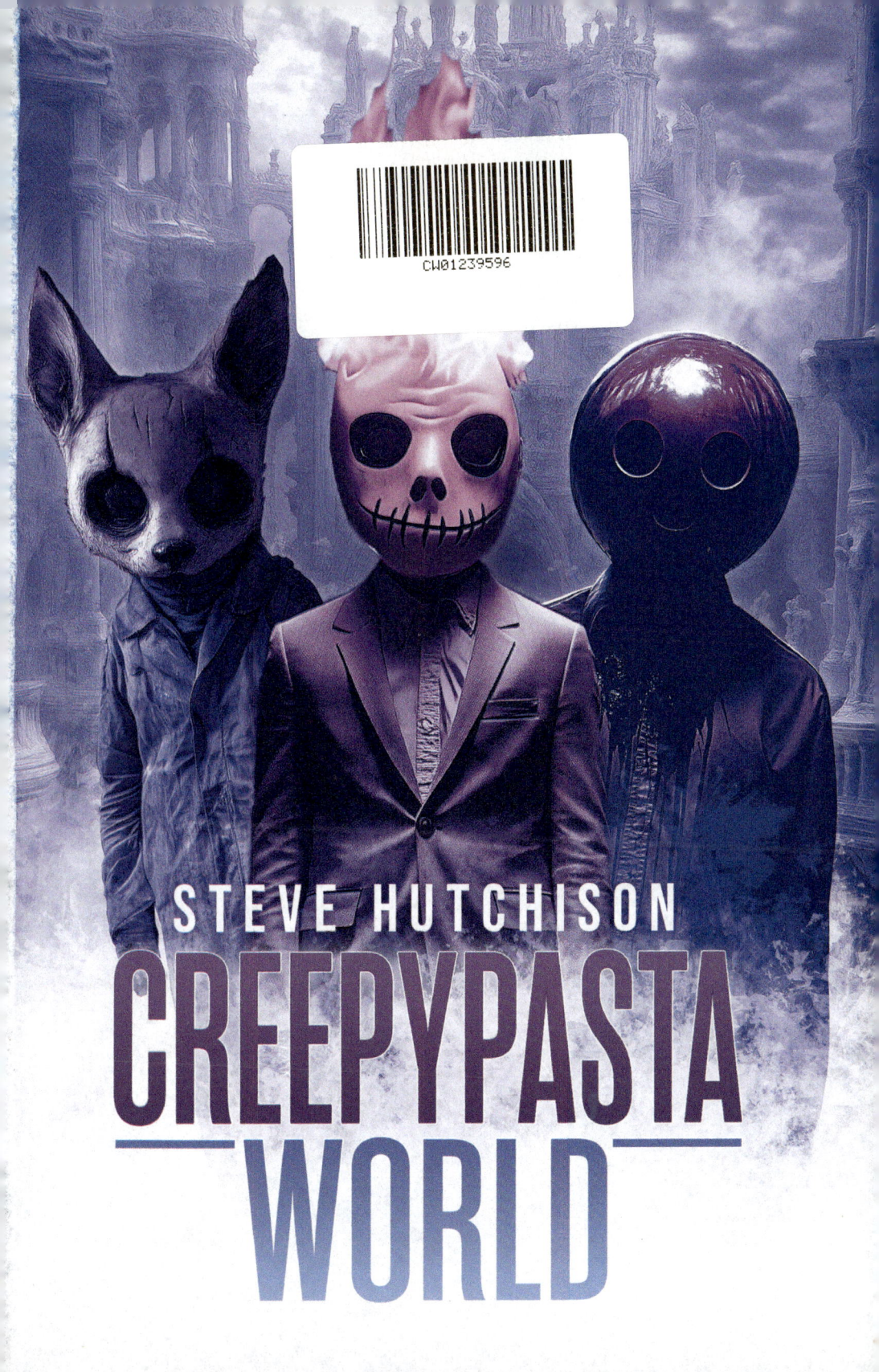

STEVE HUTCHISON
CREEPYPASTA WORLD

Copyright © 2024 by Steve Hutchison

All rights reserved. No part of this publication may be reproduced, distributed, or transmitted in any form or by any means, including photocopying, recording, or other electronic or mechanical methods, without the prior written permission of the publisher, except in the case of brief quotations used for purposes of review, commentary, or scholarly analysis.

First Edition, 2024
ISBN-13: 978-1778872754

Published by Tales of Terror
Website: https://terror.ca
Social Media: @terrorca

Steve Hutchison – steve@shade.ca
Bookstores and wholesalers: Please contact books@terror.ca

PREFACE

Welcome to Creepypasta World. What you're about to read are 20 of my most chilling stories, originally shared as viral prompts online to test how far fear could spread. The response was overwhelming, and what began as short, unsettling snippets quickly captivated readers everywhere. Now, they've been fully developed and reworked into complete stories, each one designed to pull you deeper into the darkness.

Each story is illustrated to heighten the atmosphere, drawing you into a world where nothing is quite as it seems. From psychological terror to supernatural nightmares, these tales will leave you questioning what's real long after you've finished reading. As you journey through Creepypasta World, you'll see how the line between imagination and reality can blur in ways that make you second-guess everything around you.

I hope these stories haunt you, just as they once haunted me. Enjoy the journey, and proceed with caution.

Steve Hutchison

STORIES

7. Hair Ball

13. Strawberry Rush

19. Josh Bowling

25. Puppet Room

31. Flame Stalker

37. Crystal Prison

43. Dazzle Deal

49. Celestial Escape

55. Aquatic Fascination

61. Cat Dog

67. Jelly Feast

73. Santa Hell

79. Karmic Debt

85. Pretty Please

91. Finger Eater

97. Closet Dweller

103. Imaginary Fiends

109. Endless Confinement

115. Secret Life

121. Final Episode

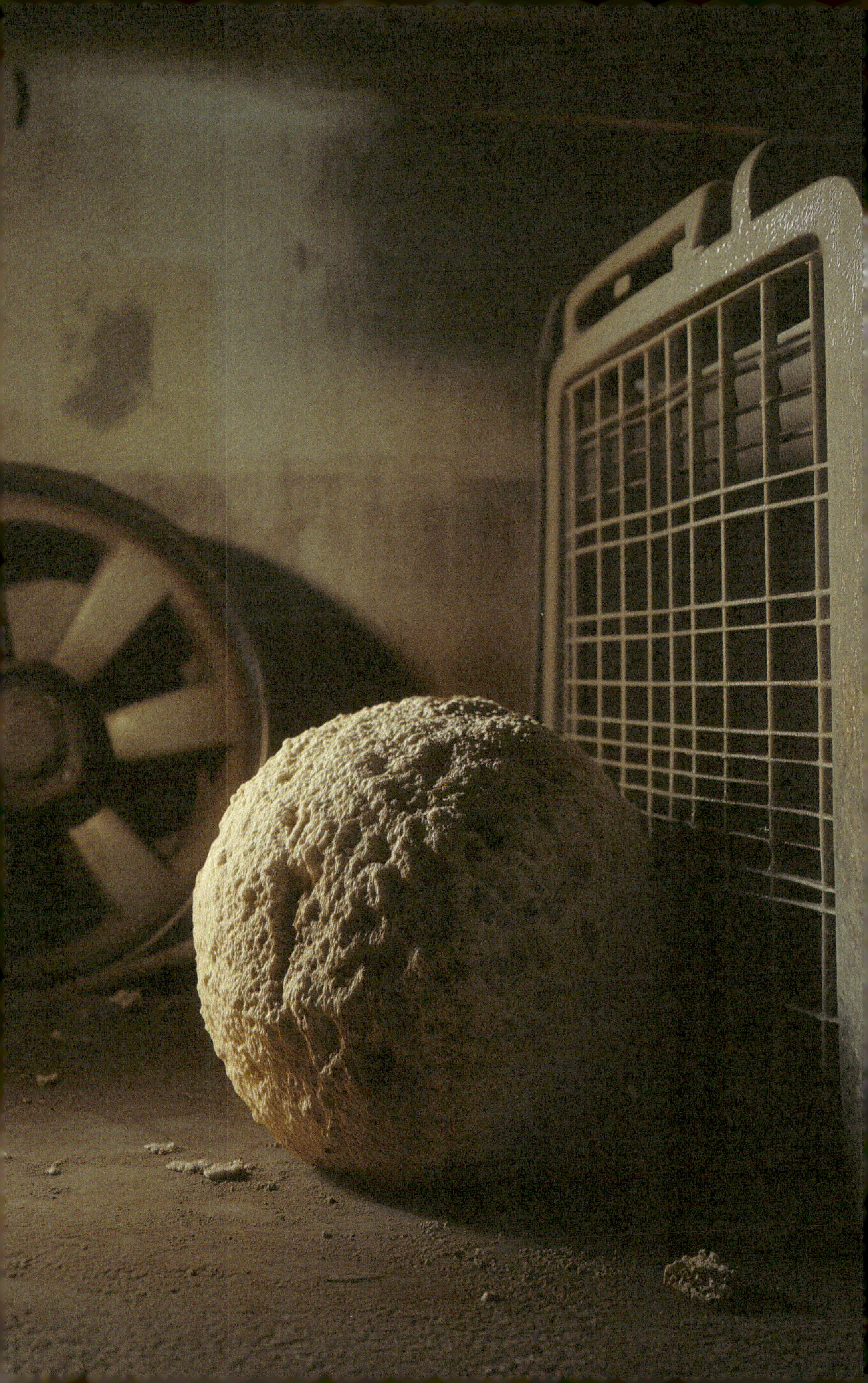

Hair Ball

One night, home alone while his mother was away on a trip, Matthew stumbled upon a bizarre ball of skin in his garage. The moment he picked it up, he was disgusted to realize it was warm and felt disturbingly alive beneath his fingers. The skin was mottled and wrinkled, making his stomach churn. He poked it with a screwdriver, but it didn't react. He poked again and this time pierced a hole. Expecting some sort of reaction, he was surprised when it remained eerily still.

Curious and feeling a mix of dread and fascination, he brought it inside. He grabbed a kitchen knife and attempted to dissect it on the counter. As he made the first cut, a lump of hair spilled out from what looked like an egg. The sight was revolting. Matthew snapped a few pictures and texted them to his girlfriend, Beth, asking her to come over and see what he'd found—though he didn't provide any details. Grossed out but intrigued, Beth replied quickly, saying she would drop by after her shift.

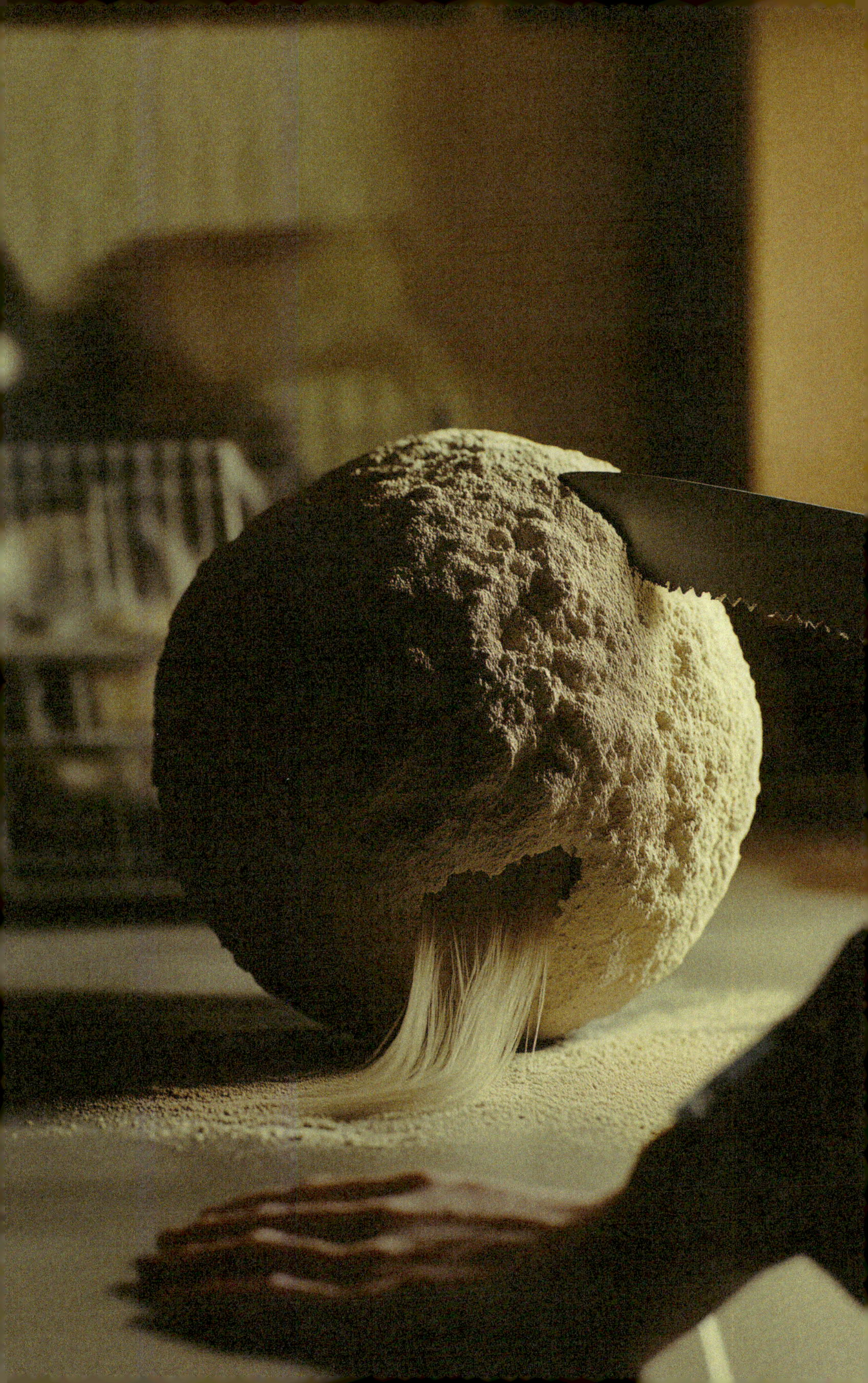

While he waited, Matthew sat on the couch, trying to focus on a movie, but his eyes kept drifting back to the strange egg. He noticed that more hair seemed to be growing from the grotesque thing, clinging to the edges like weeds. Disgusted but unable to look away, he pried the slit open wider, revealing an unsettling amount of hair packed inside. The longer he stared, the more he felt an unshakable sense of unease, as if it were watching him.

That night, Matthew couldn't stop scratching—his scalp, his ears, even his eyes. It felt as though something was crawling beneath his skin. Worried that he might be coming down with something, he tried to distract himself by watching a stand-up comedy show. He laughed for a while, but a persistent sensation of something lodged in his throat gnawed at him all evening. He drank glass after glass of water, but the feeling wouldn't go away.

He fell asleep that night, waiting for Beth to arrive, the darkness of the room swallowing him whole. As he drifted into unconsciousness, he was haunted by a sense of foreboding that wrapped around him like a shroud. As he slept, the hair began to grow uncontrollably, slithering and curling its way through the house like a sinister vine. It crept along the walls and ceilings, reaching for him as if it possessed a mind of its own.

When Matthew finally woke, he found himself nearly paralyzed, his limbs heavy and unresponsive, as if the very darkness around him had come alive. His mind was foggy, and

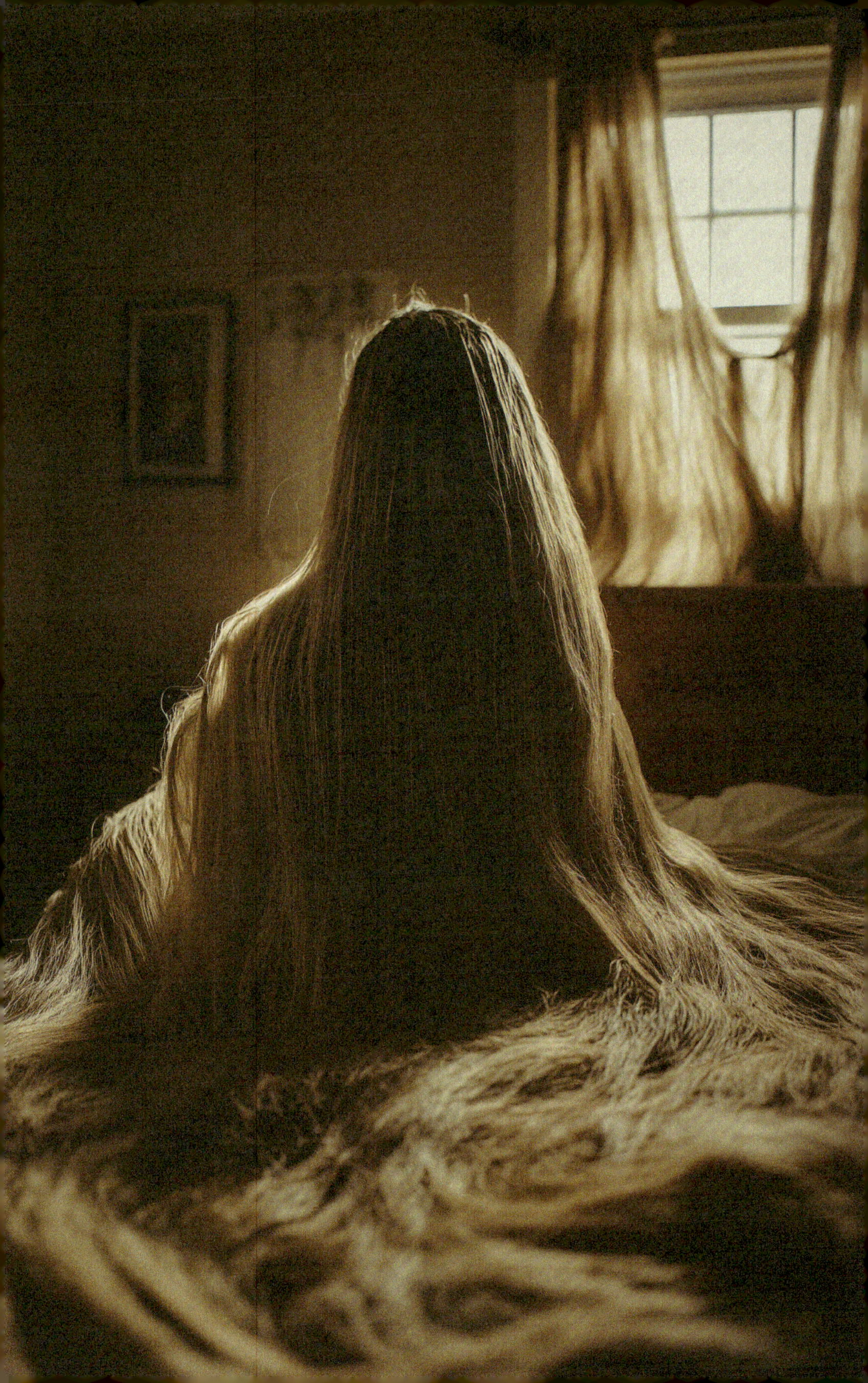

in those disorienting moments, he struggled to remember where he was and how he had fallen asleep. Panic surged through him as he felt hair tangled in his throat, choking him, its presence suffocating and invasive.

Horror washed over him as he realized he was completely engulfed in it. The warm, vibrant memories of Beth began to fade, replaced by an encroaching sense of despair. He was trapped, not only by the grotesque hair but by the fear that he might never see her again. In that crushing moment, Matthew understood the tragic irony of his situation: in his pursuit of curiosity, he had opened a door to something dark and insatiable, and now he was powerless to close it.

Later, Beth knocked and rang the doorbell, but Matthew couldn't respond. The weight of his own hair pressed down on him, making it impossible to move. With the little clarity he had left, he could barely make out Beth's voice shouting his name from the porch. Each call grew more frantic, but he was trapped, consumed by the very thing that had once intrigued him.

As the realization dawned on him, Matthew understood that he might never escape this nightmare. The grotesque ball of skin had unleashed something dark and insatiable within him, and all he could do was hope Beth would find him before it was too late.

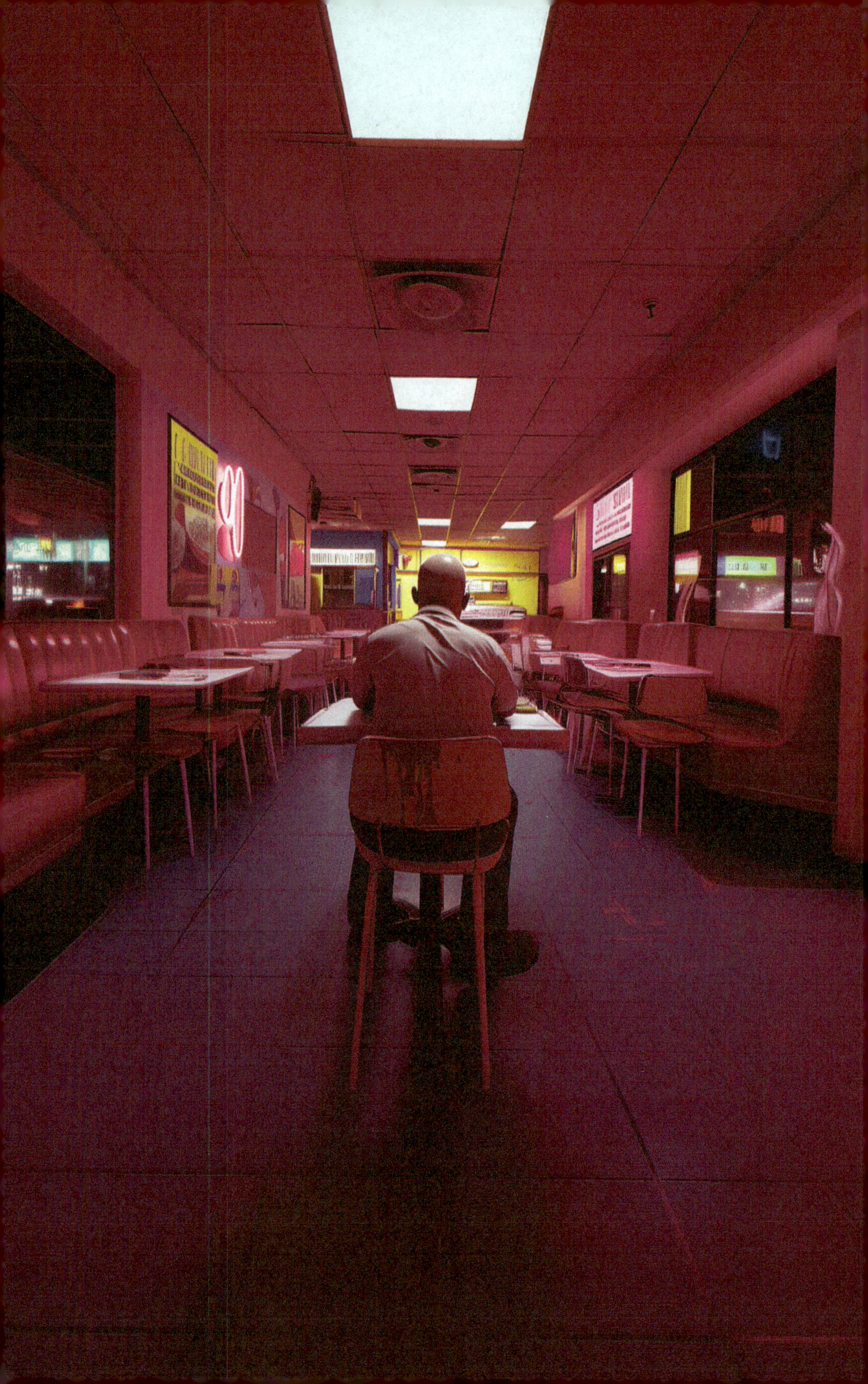

Strawberry Rush

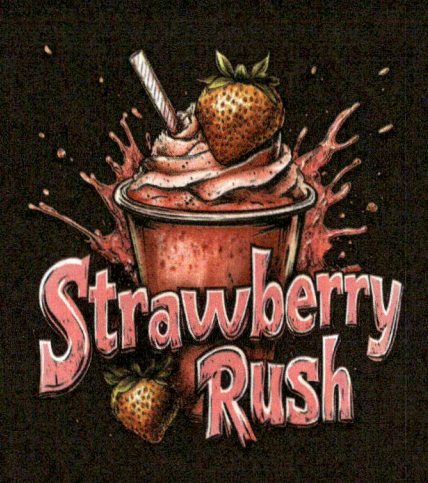

Dan owned a 1950s-inspired diner, and every Friday night, a strange man would come in, order a strawberry milkshake, and sit for hours, staring blankly at the wall. He never touched his drink, never spoke—just sat there, motionless. At first, Dan found it odd, but over time, he noticed that regulars stopped coming in on Fridays, and those who did kept glancing at the man with unease.

One night, Dan caught Walter, his employee, wiping down tables with an uneasy expression. "You know, that guy's got people a little freaked out," Walter muttered, glancing toward the man's booth. "He just... sits there like a statue. Smells strange, too."

Dan hesitated. The man was harmless, but his presence cast a chill over the place. Reluctantly, Dan decided to say something. He approached the man, cleared his throat, and spoke quietly. "Sir, if you're not ordering anything else, I'm afraid I'll have to ask you to leave."

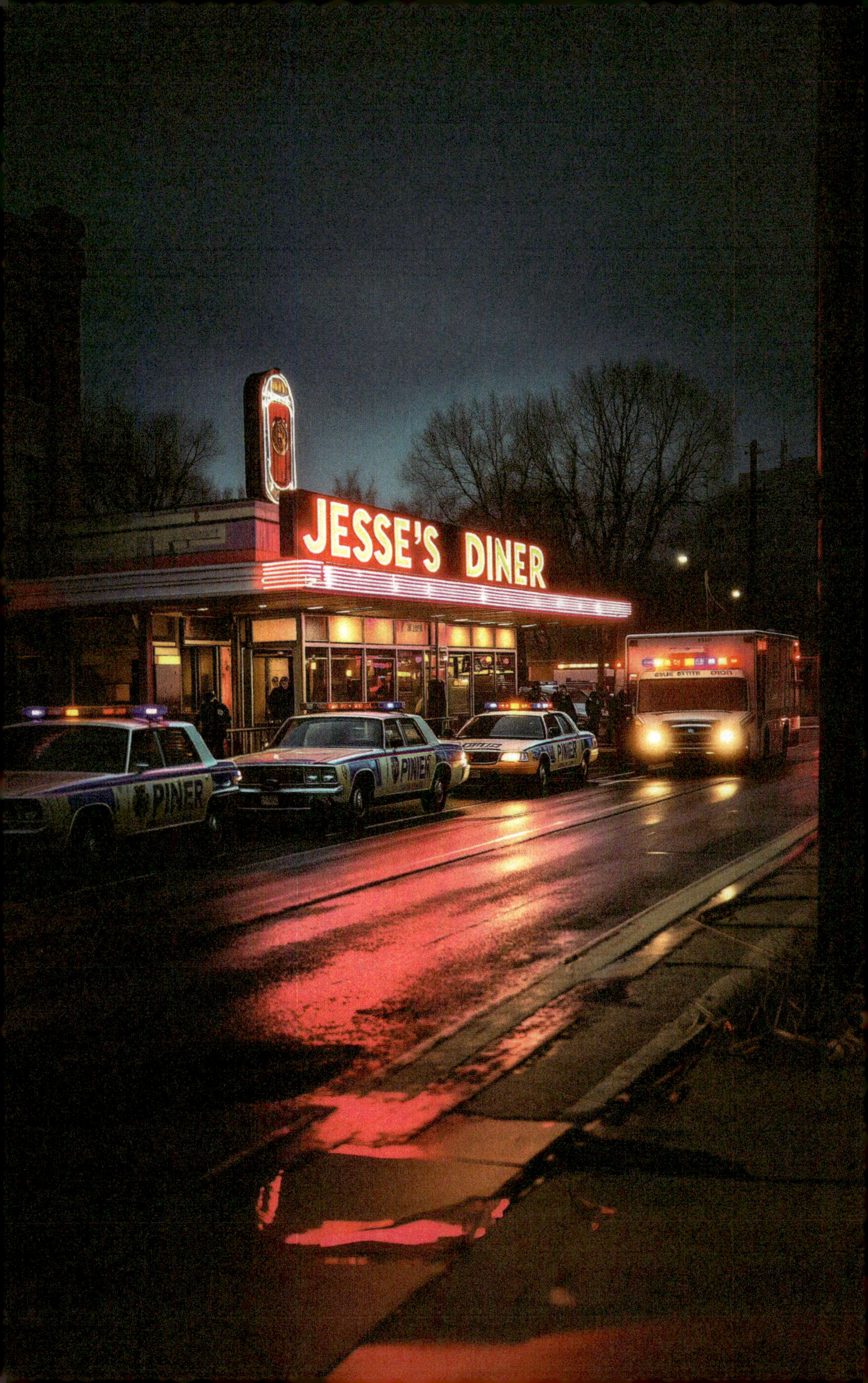
JESSE'S DINER
PINER
PINER
PINER

The man didn't react, didn't look up. He only stood, slowly, and without a word, drifted out of the diner. Dan watched as he crossed the street, feeling a strange sense of relief—until he heard a sickening thud. A car hit the man with brutal force, and he was killed instantly. Dan couldn't shake the hollow feeling in his gut, wondering if he'd somehow pushed the man to his death.

The next Friday, Dan stayed home, trying to shake off the memory. But late that night, he got a call from Walter, who sounded panicked. "Dan, you need to come back here. The guy's... he's back, and there's something really wrong."

Dan felt a chill creep up his spine as he rushed to the diner. When he stepped inside, he saw Walter, pale and shaking, staring at the man in the corner booth. The man was back, sitting in his usual spot, but he looked... changed. His skin was pale and waxy, his eyes hollow, like a corpse propped up in the booth.

Walter whispered, "He just grabbed his milkshake and... threw it. Splattered the wall with it."

As if on cue, the man picked up another milkshake, hurling it with furious force. Pink sludge dripped down the walls, and his eyes fixed on Dan, dark and empty. In a low, rasping voice, he growled, "Five more milkshakes."

Walter, terrified, scrambled to make more. The man only grew more agitated, throwing each milkshake against the walls, each impact sending pink streaks down the chrome

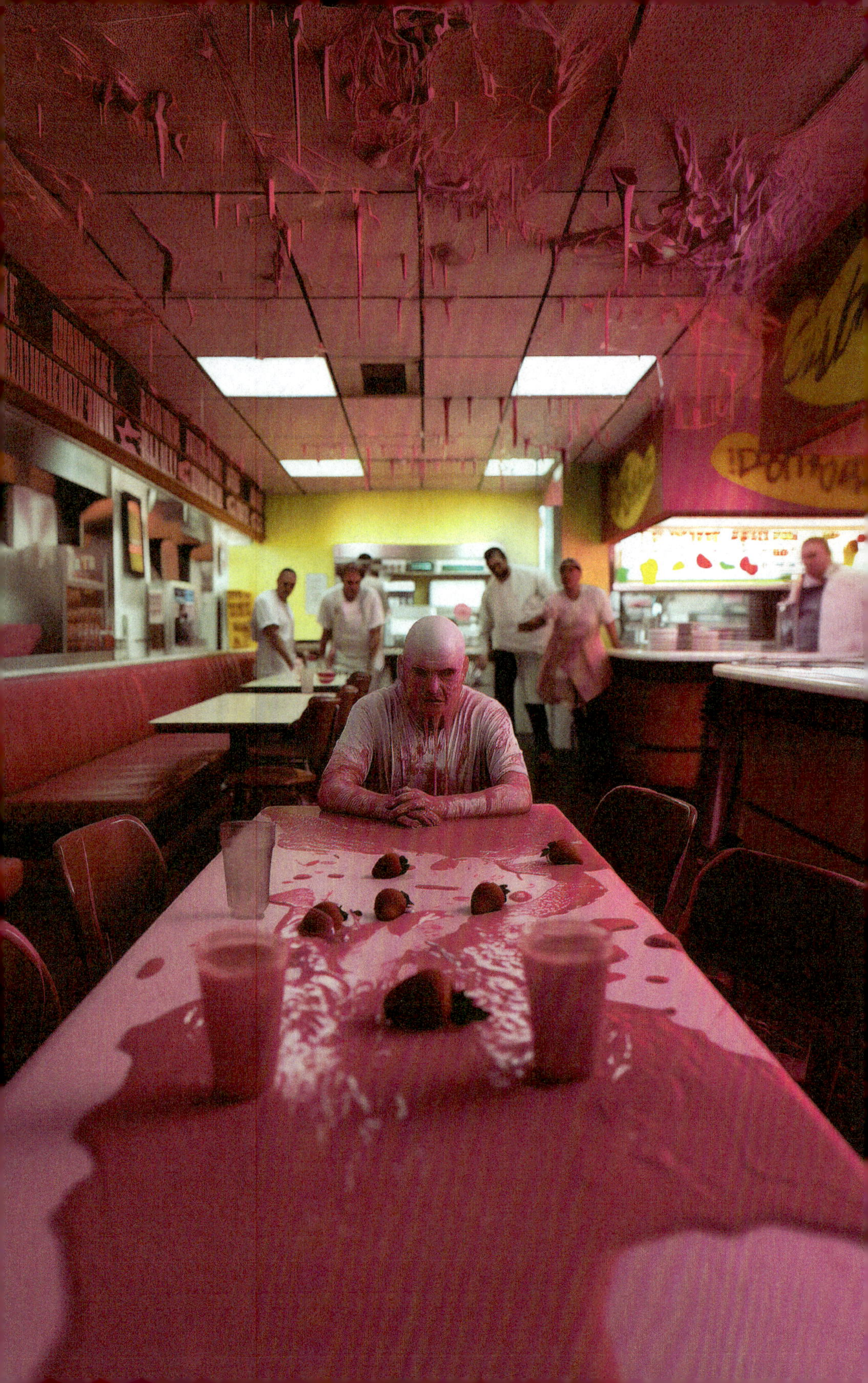

and tile. The diner transformed into a nightmare, the sticky sludge covering everything—the walls, the counters, even dripping from the ceiling. The floor was coated in strawberry pink, making it slick and treacherous.

"Five more!" he roared, his eyes locked on Dan.

Dan stood frozen, watching as Walter made the final batch, the man hurling each with a wild, terrible intensity. By the end, the diner was drenched in strawberry sludge, the cheerful décor twisted into something horrific. The place had turned into a grotesque, sticky nightmare.

The man finally stopped, slumping back in his seat, his eyes returning to the wall. In a voice that barely sounded human, he whispered, "More milkshake…"

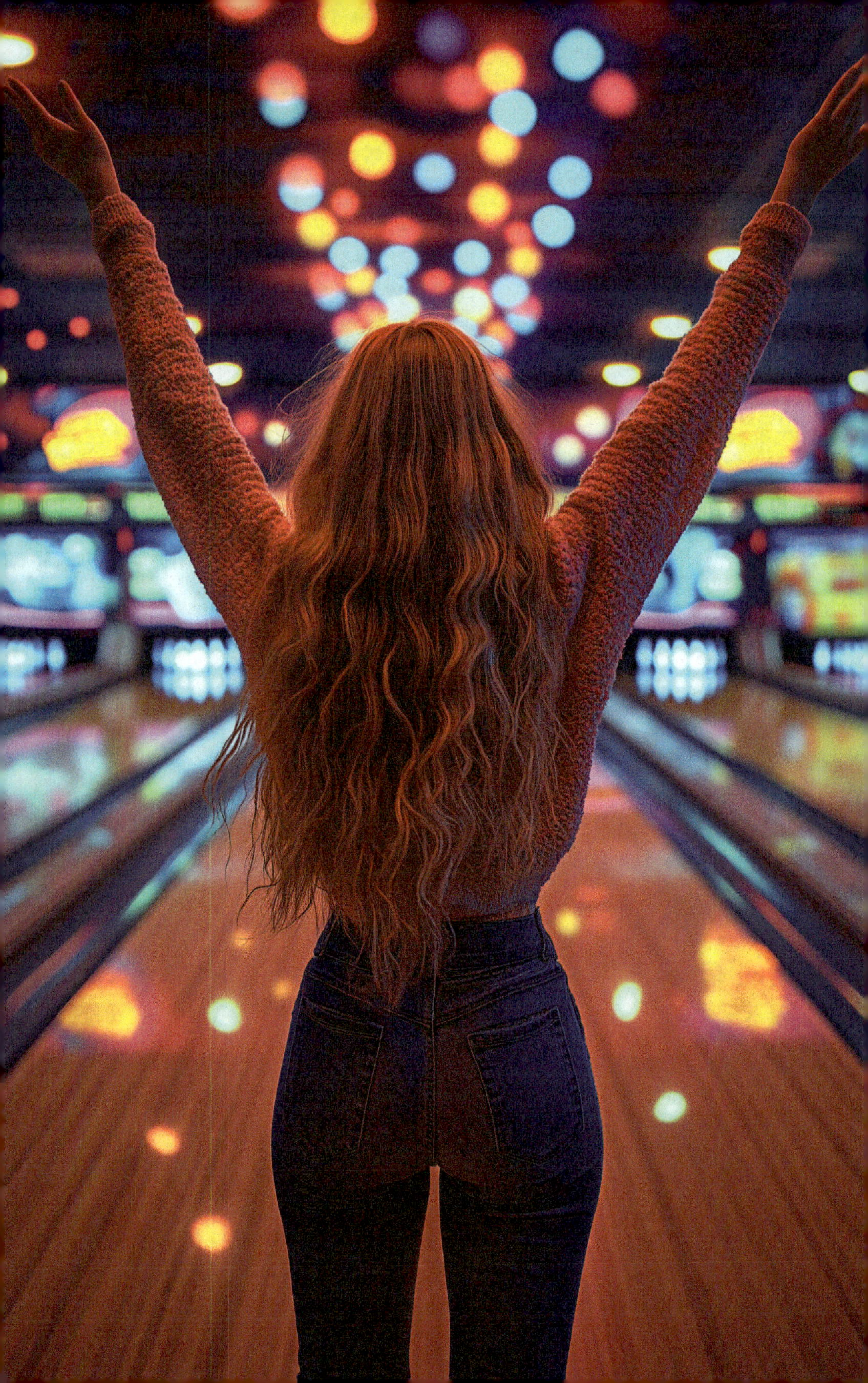

Josh Bowling

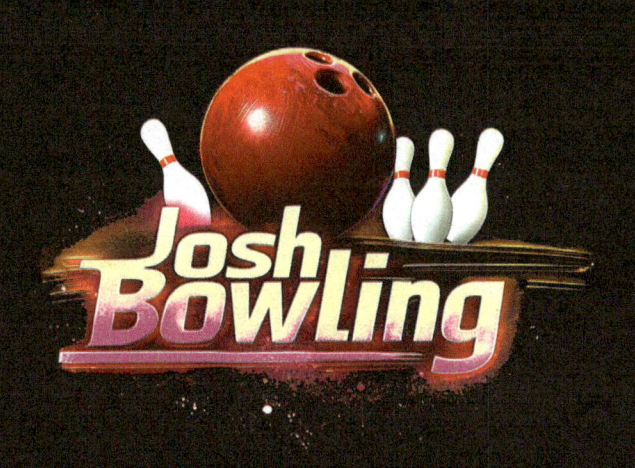

Jennica and her friends buzzed with excitement as they approached the famous bowling center rumored to be haunted. The tale of a mysterious figure—a man with a bowling ball for a head—had kept the place alive for years, attracting thrill-seekers.

As someone who had worked as a haunted-walk organizer, Jennica scoffed at the idea but couldn't deny her curiosity for a good scare.

Once inside, the energy surged. Jennica was on fire, knocking down pins with ease as her friends cheered her on. After a few games and a round of beers, she glanced at the scoreboard with pride—she was winning.

"Where's Matt?" Jennica asked, scanning the bustling alley.

Tammy, Matt's girlfriend, frowned. "He went to the men's room a while ago. Maybe he's outside having a smoke."

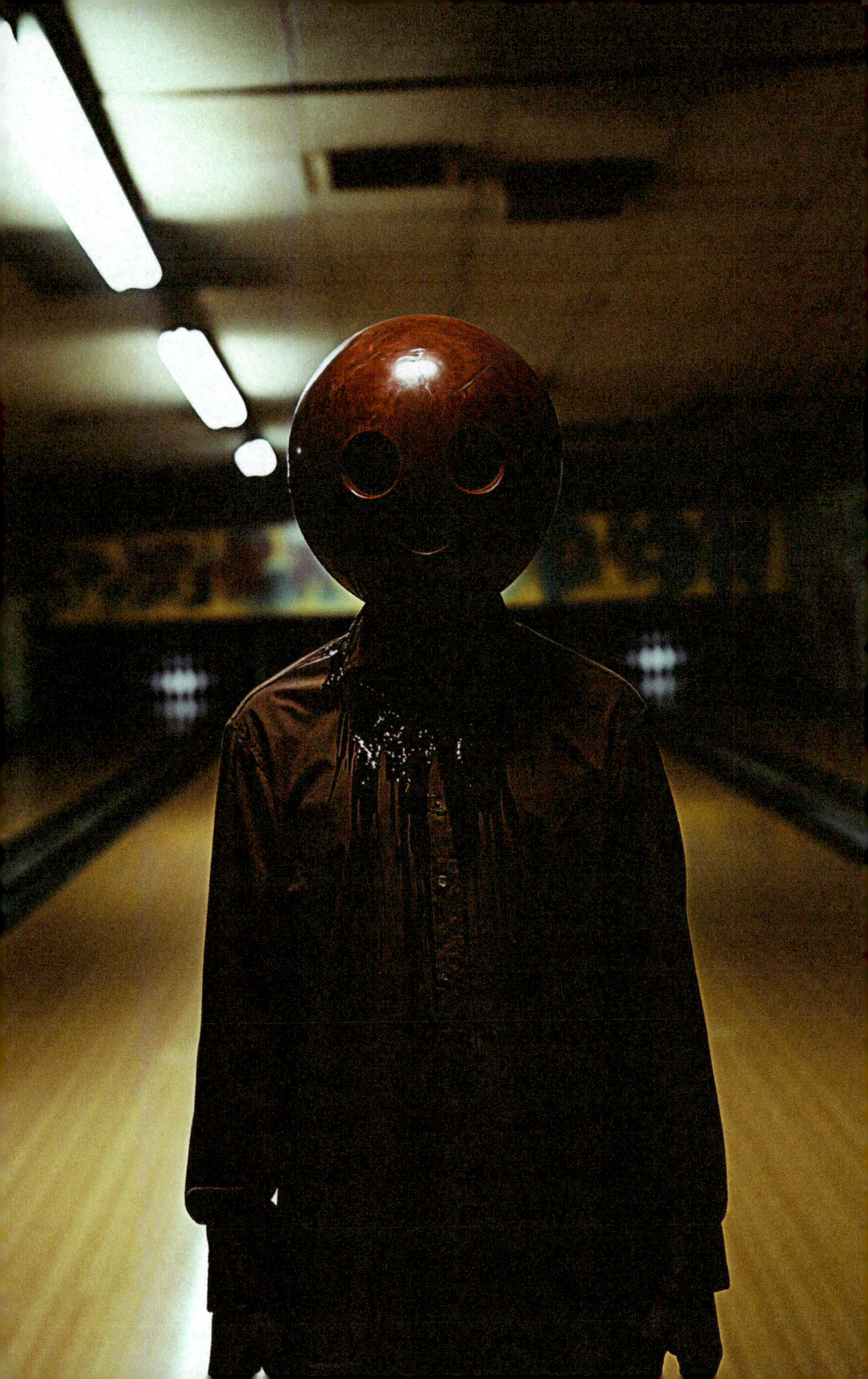

As the laughter and banter continued, Jennica felt a twinge of worry. Matt had been gone longer than expected. She glanced at the clock, then around the room, searching for him.

Meanwhile, Matt had wandered away from the group, drawn toward the dim hallway leading to the abandoned wing of the bowling center. A flicker of something red caught his eye, pulling him deeper into the shadows.

"Just a little peek," he told himself, dismissing the unease creeping up his spine. The hallway was eerily quiet, the air thick with tension. He hesitated at the door at the end of the corridor, then flicked on the lights.

In the flickering glow, a figure emerged—a terrifying man with a bowling ball for a head. Matt's heart raced as he noticed something disturbing seeping from the holes in its face. Fear surged through him, and he stumbled back, struggling to process the horror.

Suddenly, the figure lunged, and everything went dark.

Back at the bowling alley, Jennica's concern for Matt grew. "He's been gone too long," she said, glancing at the clock. Just then, she noticed the ball return machine whirring to life. Curious, she leaned closer, expecting to see her bright bowling ball. Instead, her heart dropped as recognition struck her like lightning.

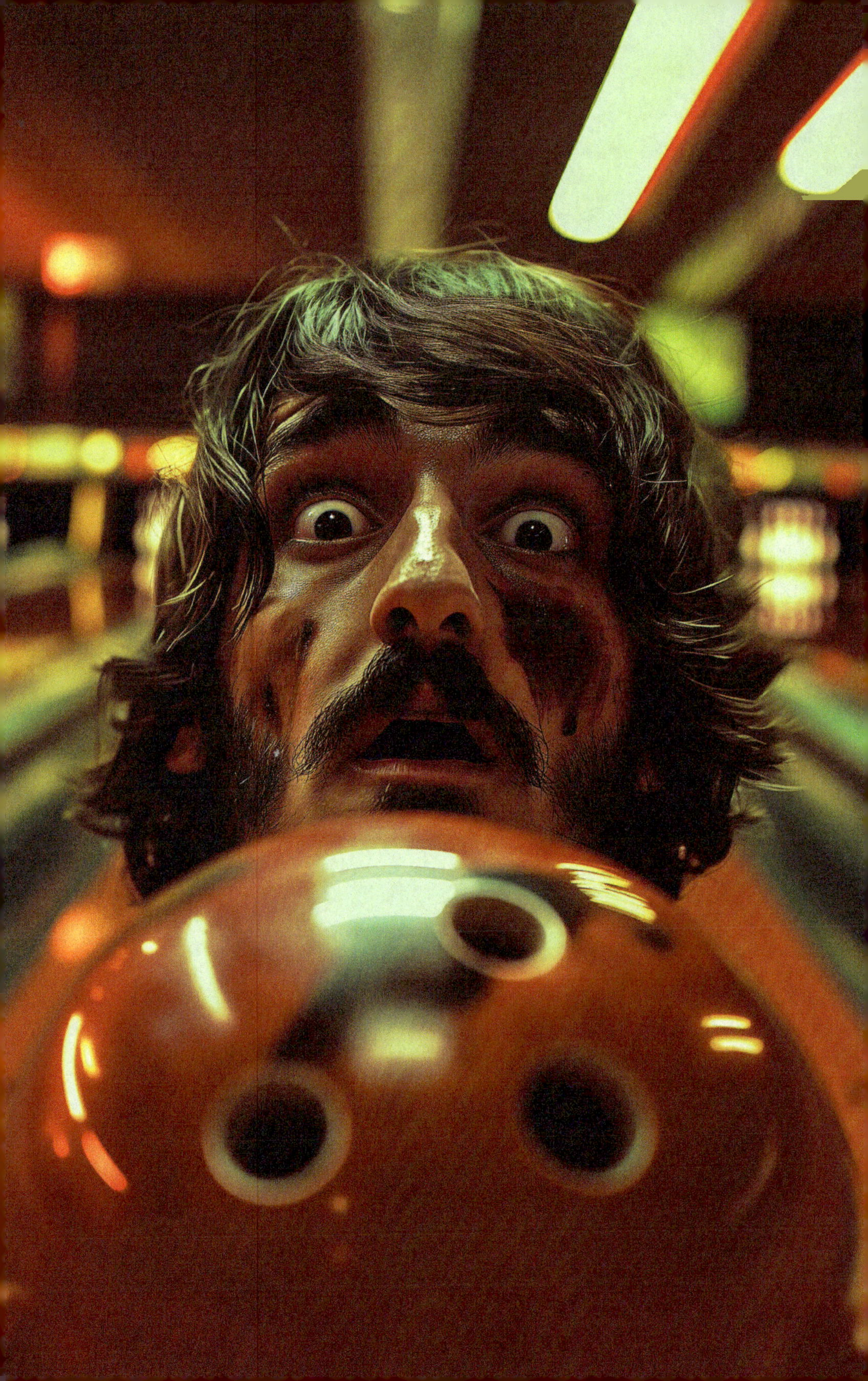

It wasn't her ball; it was a round, dark object that sent chills down her spine. It was Matt's head—eerily familiar, lifeless, and still.

"Matt?" she whispered, her voice trembling as dread crashed down on her. The laughter of her friends faded into a chilling silence. She stumbled back, panic rising as the lights flickered, casting twisted shadows along the walls. The reality of the legend hit her—Josh Bowling was real, and the sight of her friend confirmed it.

Without thinking, she turned and ran for the nearest exit, never to return.

Days turned into years, and she would warn others about the bowling center, but no one believed her. They pretended to listen, yet the thrill of the legend was too enticing to dismiss. Deep down, Jennica knew Josh Bowling was still waiting for the next unsuspecting victim to step into the darkness.

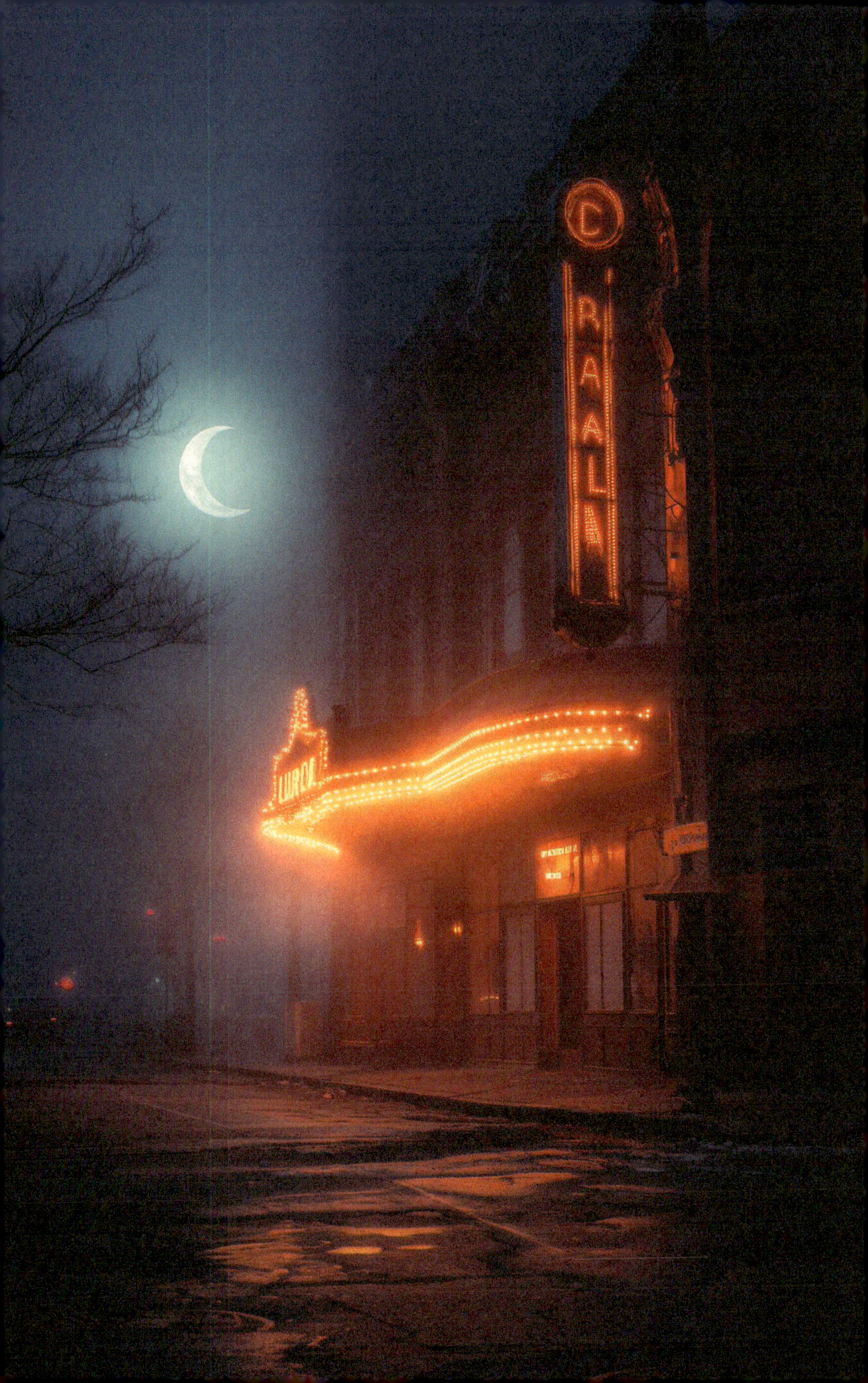

Puppet Room

James Holloway, a seasoned cultural critic for a prominent newspaper, received a curious invitation to a puppet show in a small, obscure room called The Velvet Curtain. The note had been simple yet intriguing: "This screening is exclusive—only one critic at a time." Intrigued by the promise of something unique, he made his way to the venue, an unassuming brick building with peeling paint and a flickering sign.

As he parked his car and stepped inside the building, he was immediately enveloped by a thick fog that clung to the ground in the dimly lit hallway, swirling around his ankles as he walked. The damp air had an eerie quality, and he found himself glancing over his shoulder, as if he were being watched. He scanned the surroundings for cameras or any sign of an audience observing him from the shadows. The unsettling feeling lingered as he pushed open the heavy door to the old theater, stepping into a narrow hallway. The fog curled mysteriously around the edges of the light fixtures

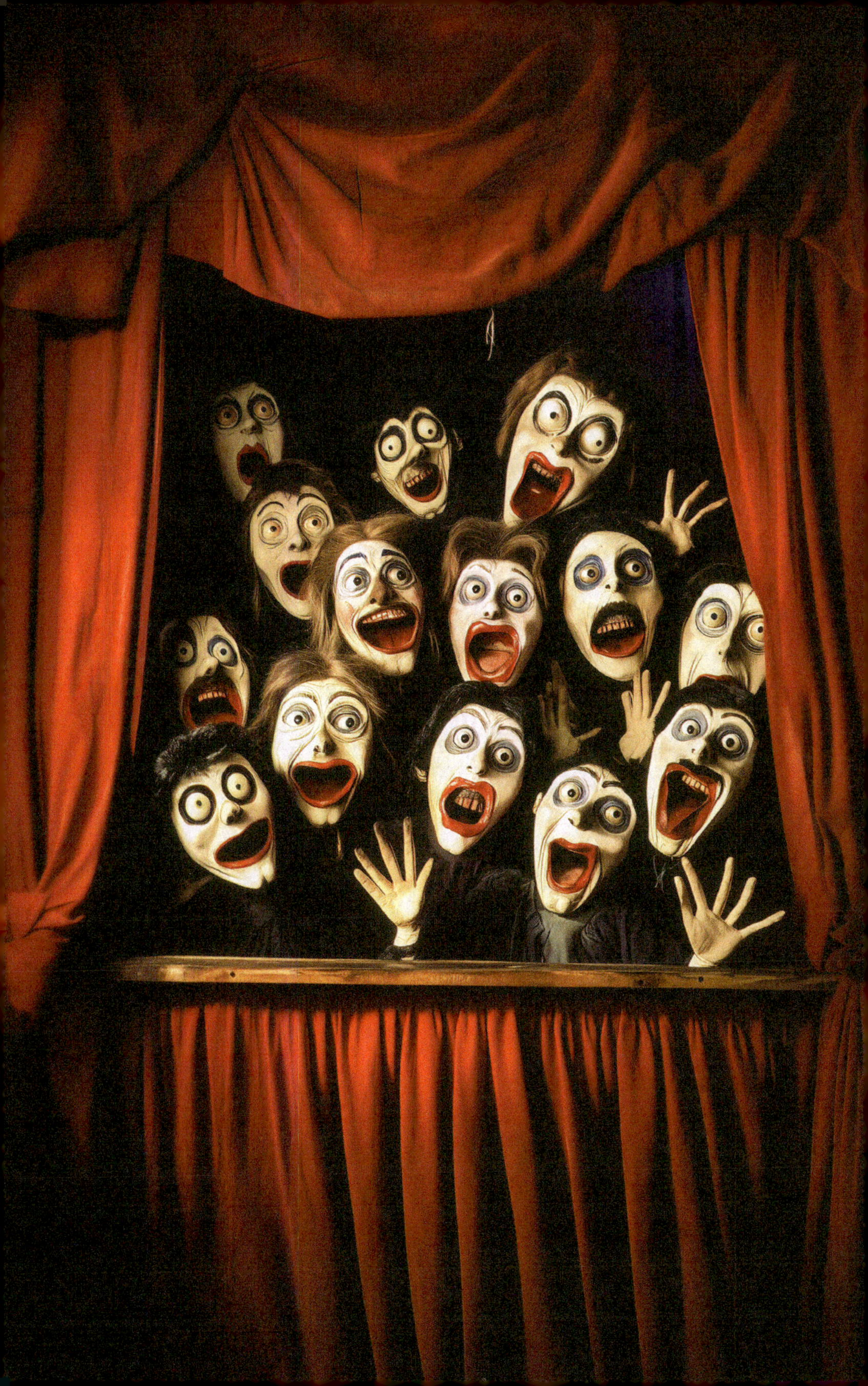

overhead, making him wonder if they had used a smoke machine to enhance the atmosphere.

As he entered the dimly lit space, an unsettling chill crept over him. The atmosphere was thick with anticipation, and the faint scent of dust mingled with something sweetly rotten. In the center of the room stood a small puppet stage, surrounded by long red velvet curtains that seemed to close in around him. On the stage, the puppets awaited—an assortment of grotesque figures crafted from crumpled paper, their expressions frozen in sinister grins.

James felt an irresistible urge to sit down as if the puppets were beckoning him to watch. He settled into a worn velvet chair in the front row. As the curtains parted slowly, the show began.

At first, it seemed like an innocuous performance, but as the puppets started to move, he couldn't shake the impression that they were speaking directly to him. They whispered and giggled among themselves, their beady eyes flicking toward him as if sharing secrets. With every twist and turn of the story, they painted a disturbing picture of his life—his successes, failures, and even his private thoughts.

James's heart raced as the performance escalated. He shifted uneasily in his seat, feeling exposed under the scrutiny of these paper figures. Just as he began to question his own sanity, he glanced around the empty room, hoping to see other audience members. To his horror, he discovered that the seats to his left and right were now filled with more

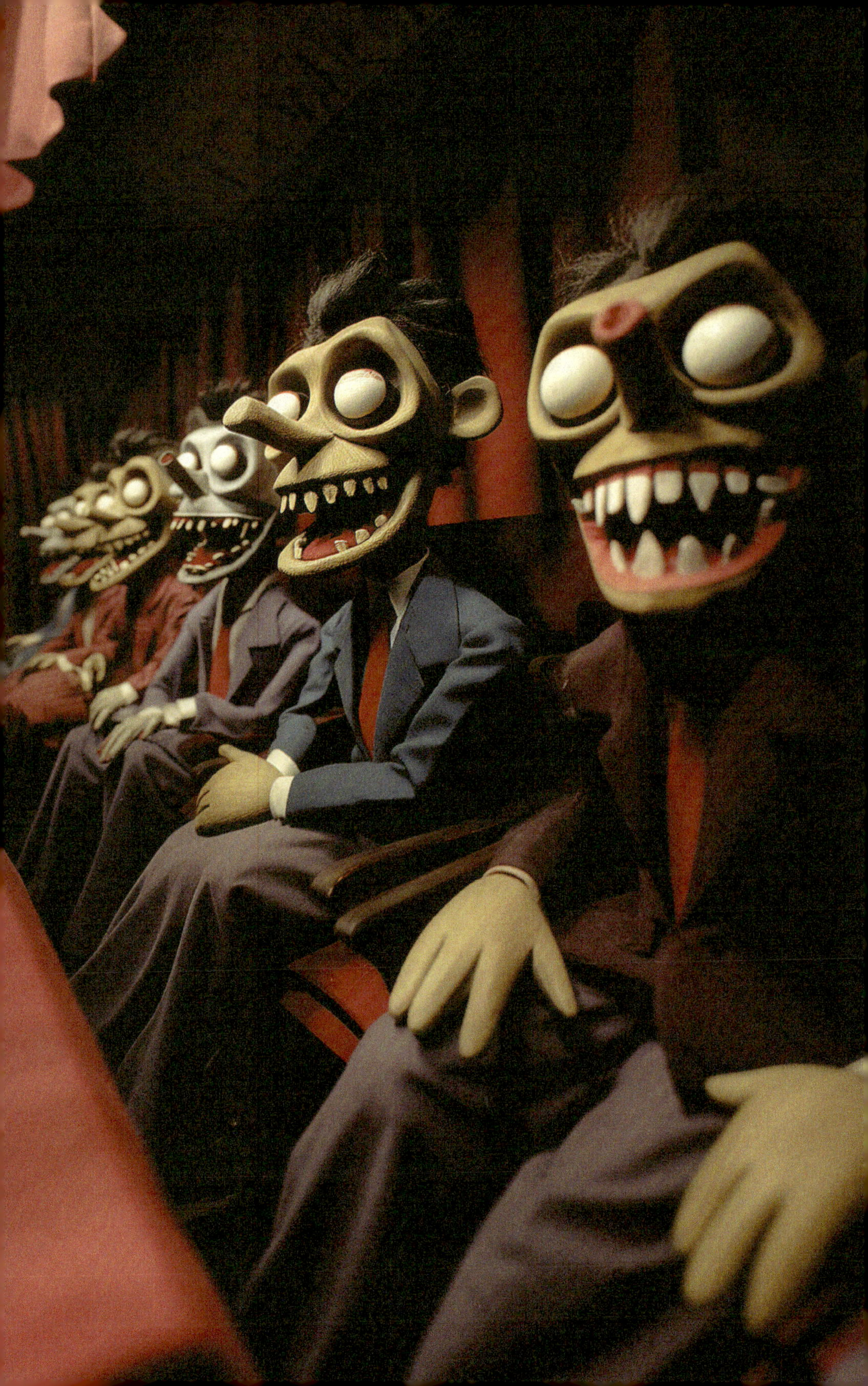

puppets—giant versions of those on stage—each one staring unblinkingly at him, their painted smiles a stark contrast to the growing dread in his chest.

A scream threatened to escape his lips, but before he could utter a sound, the puppets hushed him in unison, their voices a chilling whisper. "Shhh, you must watch," they urged, their movements becoming more animated as they closed in on him. The show morphed into a dark carnival, the puppets dancing and taunting, their laughter echoing off the walls.

Suddenly, the giant puppets beside him erupted into laughter, their enormous paper mouths opening wide. In their hands, they held small mirrors, each one reflecting his image back at him. James's heart dropped as he saw himself—a paper puppet just like them, his own features crudely drawn and lifeless. The realization struck him: he had been a puppet all along, trapped in a twisted performance that he could never escape.

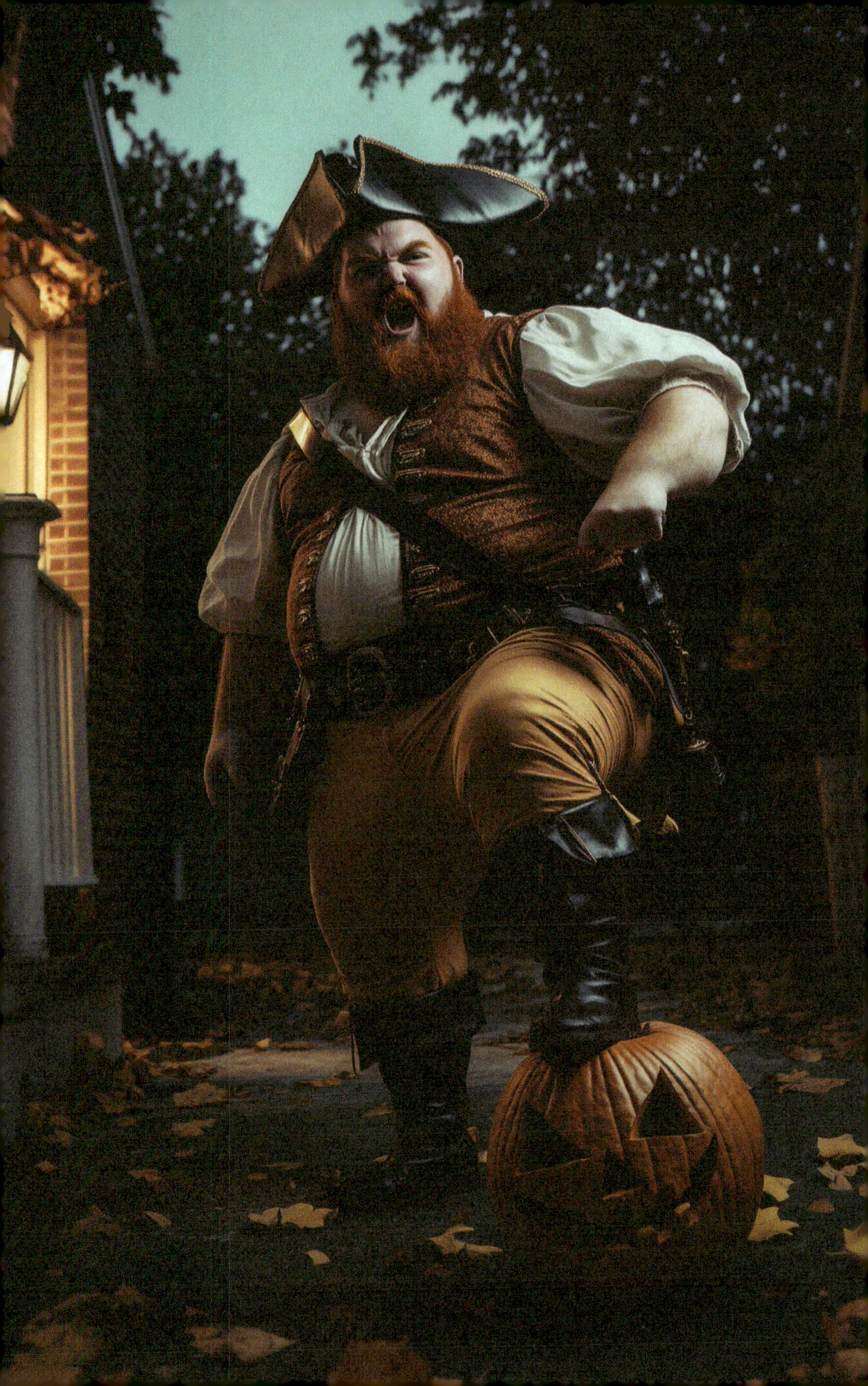

Flame Stalker

Joshua had gotten drunk at a Halloween party, only to lose the interest of the girl he had a crush on. She was the sole reason he had come, yet she barely looked his way. Joshua couldn't find the courage to approach her, let alone navigate through the wall of alpha males surrounding her. Frustrated, he walked home seething with anger, his mind clouded by self-pity. Along the way, he coerced some children into giving him candy, their parents frowning disapprovingly at his antics.

On his way, he noticed a carved pumpkin lying on the ground. In a fit of rage, he stepped on it, imagining it was the head of the guy who had stolen his date. Growling, he crushed it underfoot.

Out of the corner of his eye, Joshua spotted a figure with a burning head, flames flickering like a malevolent beacon. He wasn't sure how long the man had been watching him, but a primal instinct sent a shiver down his spine. When he

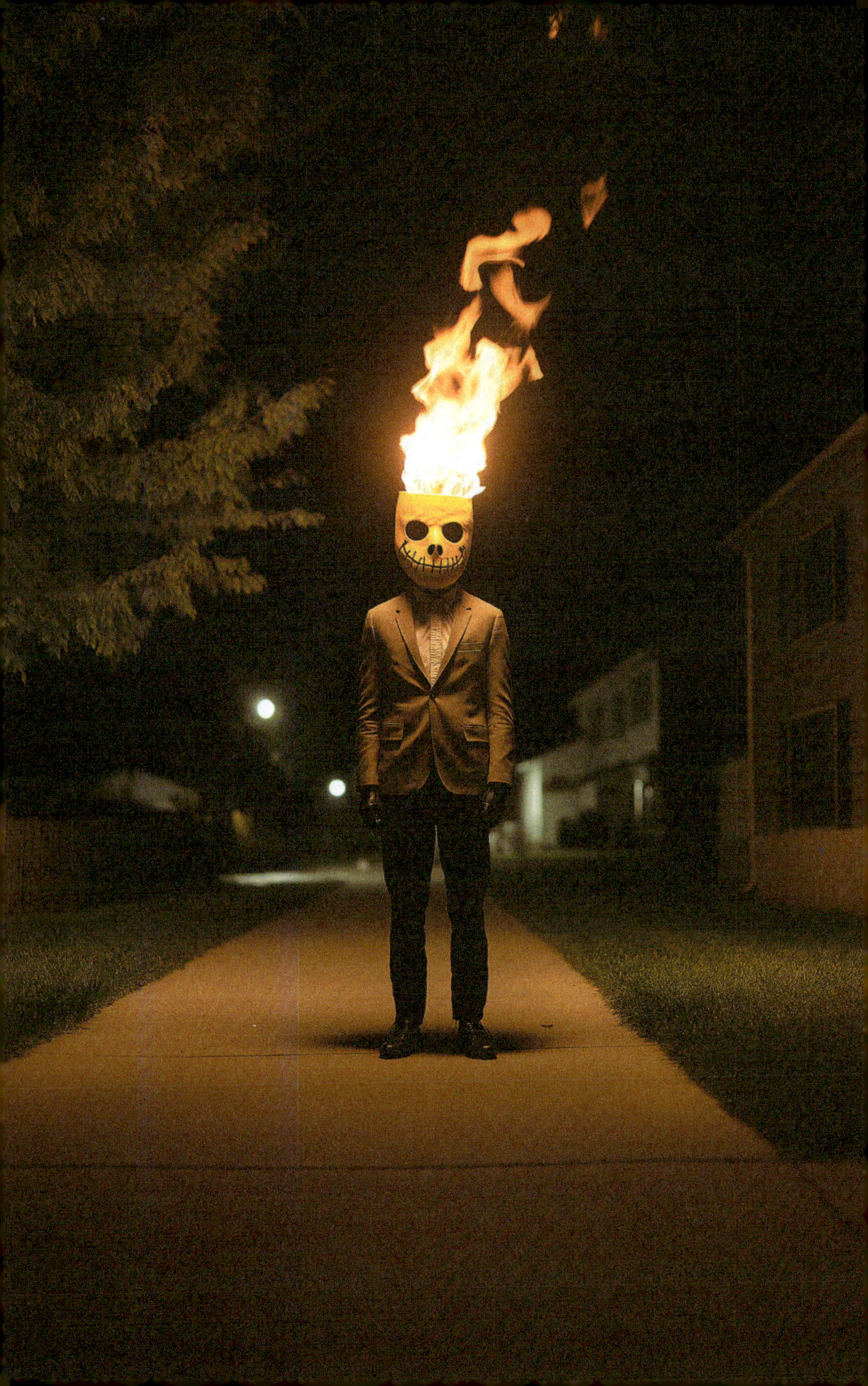

stepped forward, the man mirrored his movement, an unnerving reflection that sent adrenaline coursing through Joshua's veins.

Joshua moved left, glancing over his shoulder, but the man mirrored him with unsettling precision. Each step he took seemed to pull them closer, yet the distance remained eerily constant, as if an invisible string tethered them together. Joshua could feel the heat radiating from the figure, a stark contrast to the cool night air.

Panic bubbled inside him as he tried to escape the shadowy figure. He stepped backward, but the man followed seamlessly, his burning head casting flickering shadows across the pavement. No matter how far Joshua retreated, the figure remained steadfast, feeding off his anxiety. The air grew thick with tension, and Joshua's mind raced with thoughts of escape, but each frantic attempt only seemed to strengthen their connection.

Frustrated, Joshua finally decided to confront the man. He taunted him, dubbing him the Flamestalker, and noticed the flames on the man's head flare up in response. In a surge of anger, Joshua punched the man's mask, which flew off to reveal nothing beneath it but a blazing flame that crackled ominously. The fire twisted and churned, almost alive, as a guttural laugh echoed in the air, sending terror through Joshua.

Without a word, the Flamestalker collapsed.

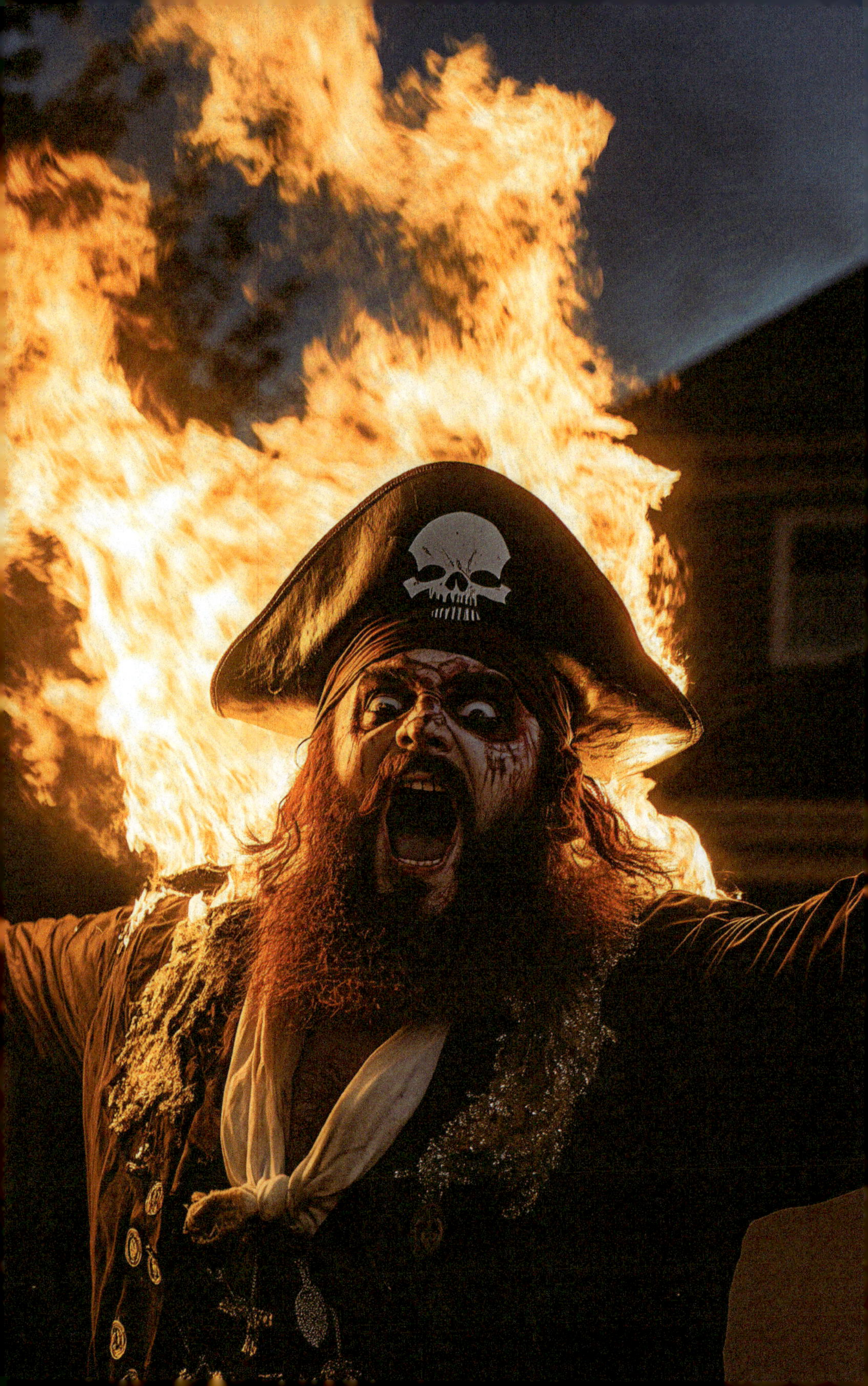

Feeling proud, Joshua bragged that it had been easy. He strutted around like a pirate, convinced of his invincibility.

But suddenly, his hat ignited, flames shooting up unexpectedly. Joshua's eyes widened in shock. Panicking, he swatted at the fire and stomped on it, managing to extinguish the flames. "That cost me $20," he muttered, looking at the charred remains.

That night, flames erupted around Joshua, wrapping him in a fierce, consuming fire. This fire crackled with a sinister life of its own, twisting and swirling as if it hungered for him. Joshua screamed, but his cries were swallowed by the night, the flames dancing higher and illuminating the darkness.

In those agonizing moments, he felt his essence stripped away, memories of his failures flashing before his eyes. The heat intensified, consuming all that he had been. With each agonizing second, he transformed, merging with the inferno until he was no longer Joshua—a drunken fool—but the Flamestalker, a harbinger of fire and vengeance.

The flames settled into a flickering crown above his head, marking him as a relentless force of wrath. From that night forward, wherever fire flickered in the dark, his presence would be felt, haunting the living and feeding on their fear.

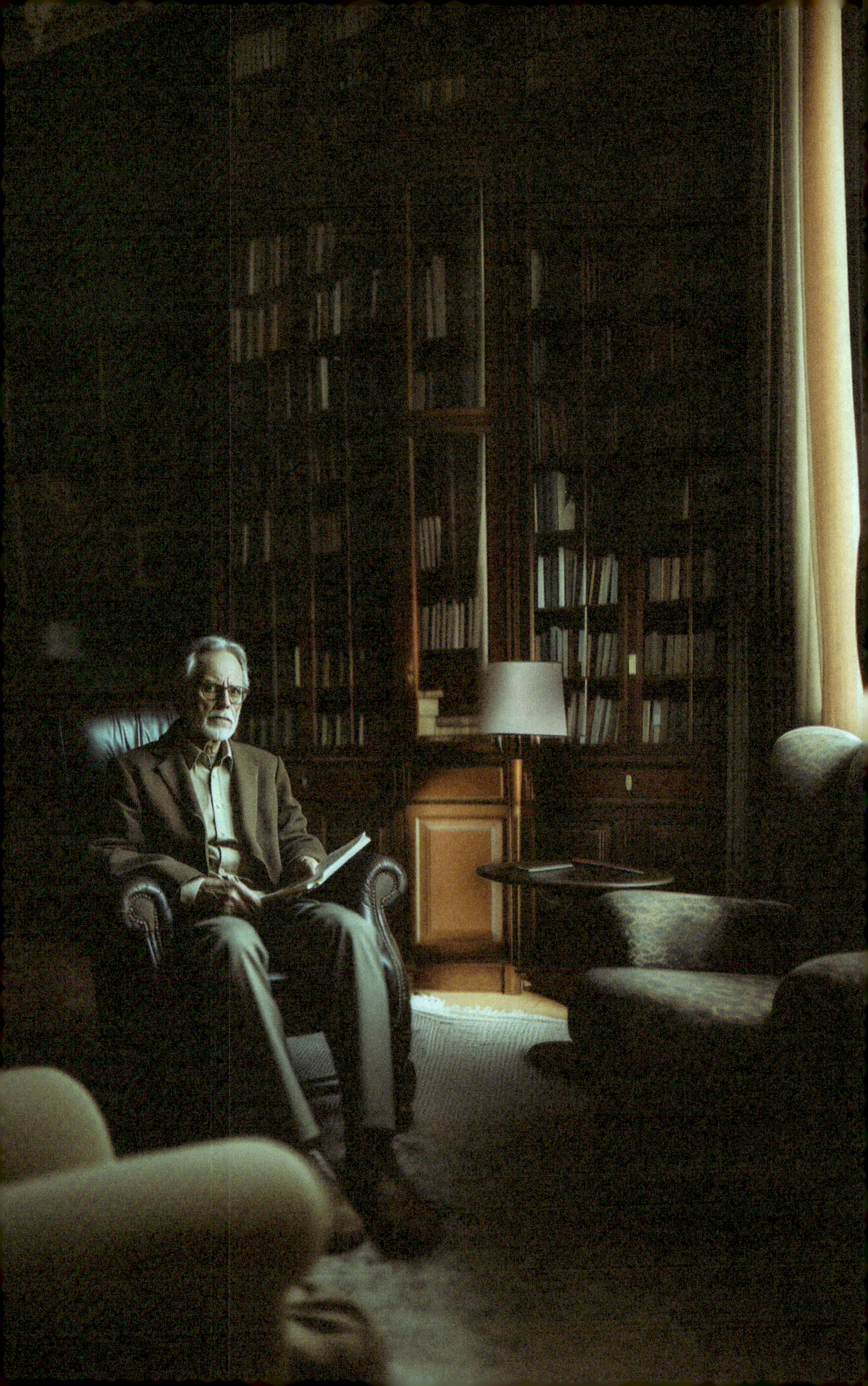

Crystal Prison

Dr. Randolph Wexler, a renowned psychiatrist, recalls an encounter from ten years ago—one that has haunted him ever since. Even now, the memory of that day remains disturbingly vivid. He remembers the moment she walked into his office—a woman whose skin shimmered, entirely covered in gemstones that caught the light from every angle. Her face was a mask of fear, and her skin formed a breathtaking patchwork of multicolored stones. She looked like a walking masterpiece—and a cursed one.

As she entered, she dropped a small velvet pouch onto his desk, its contents clinking softly against one another. The pouch held a collection of uncut gemstones—raw yet shimmering with the same strange intensity as her skin. She offered them in exchange for his help, a desperate plea to end her suffering.

Dr. Wexler listened patiently as the woman, anxious and exhausted, explained how the puppet had convinced her that

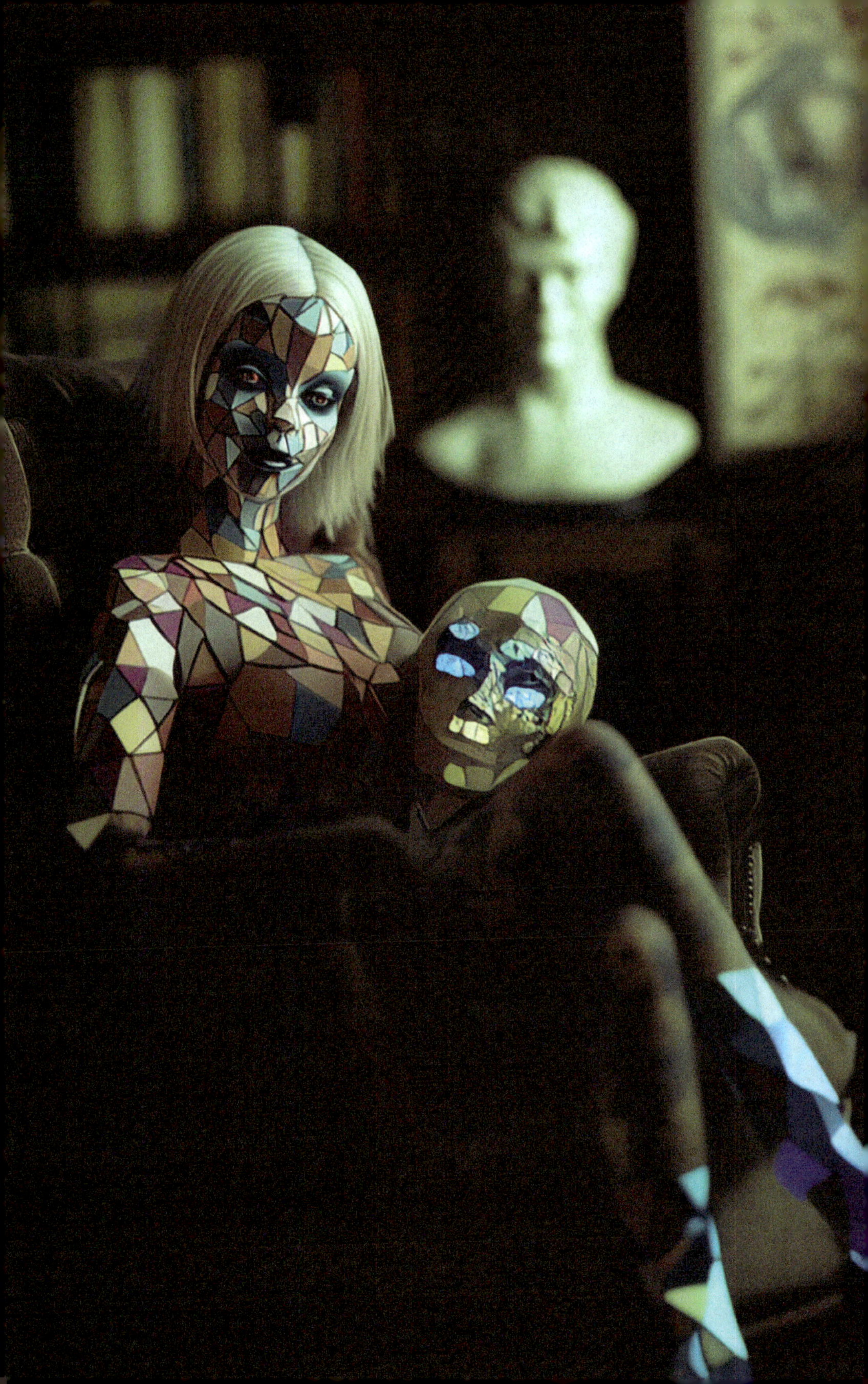

they were physically bound, a single entity. Every attempt to remove it intensified her pain, as the puppet's skin merged deeper with hers. Convinced this was a manifestation of her fear, he offered what he hoped would be empowering advice.

"Remember, it's just a puppet," he said gently. "Tell it that it has no hold over you, that it's merely an object. Then calmly remove it from your hand. You are in control here."

The woman hesitated, but her desperation soon overcame her fear. She stared into the puppet's cold, stone eyes, took a deep breath, and said firmly, "You have no hold over me."

A sudden chill swept through the room, and the puppet seemed to come alive in a way that sent shivers down her spine. Its glassy eyes glinted with an unsettling light, and she heard a soft, mocking voice echo in her mind. "Do you really think you can get rid of me? I am a part of you now. Without me, you'll be nothing but a broken shell. Let's not do this; together, we are powerful." Doubt flickered in her chest, threatening to undo her resolve.

Dr. Wexler felt it all, and for an instant, he believed the puppet was truly alive. A chill ran down his spine as he sensed its influence over the woman. He struggled to reconcile the bizarre symptoms he was witnessing with everything he had learned about the human mind. Overwhelmed by the sheer strangeness of the situation, he fought to maintain a facade of control, even as uncertainty gnawed at him. Deep down, he realized he was confronting something far beyond his understanding.

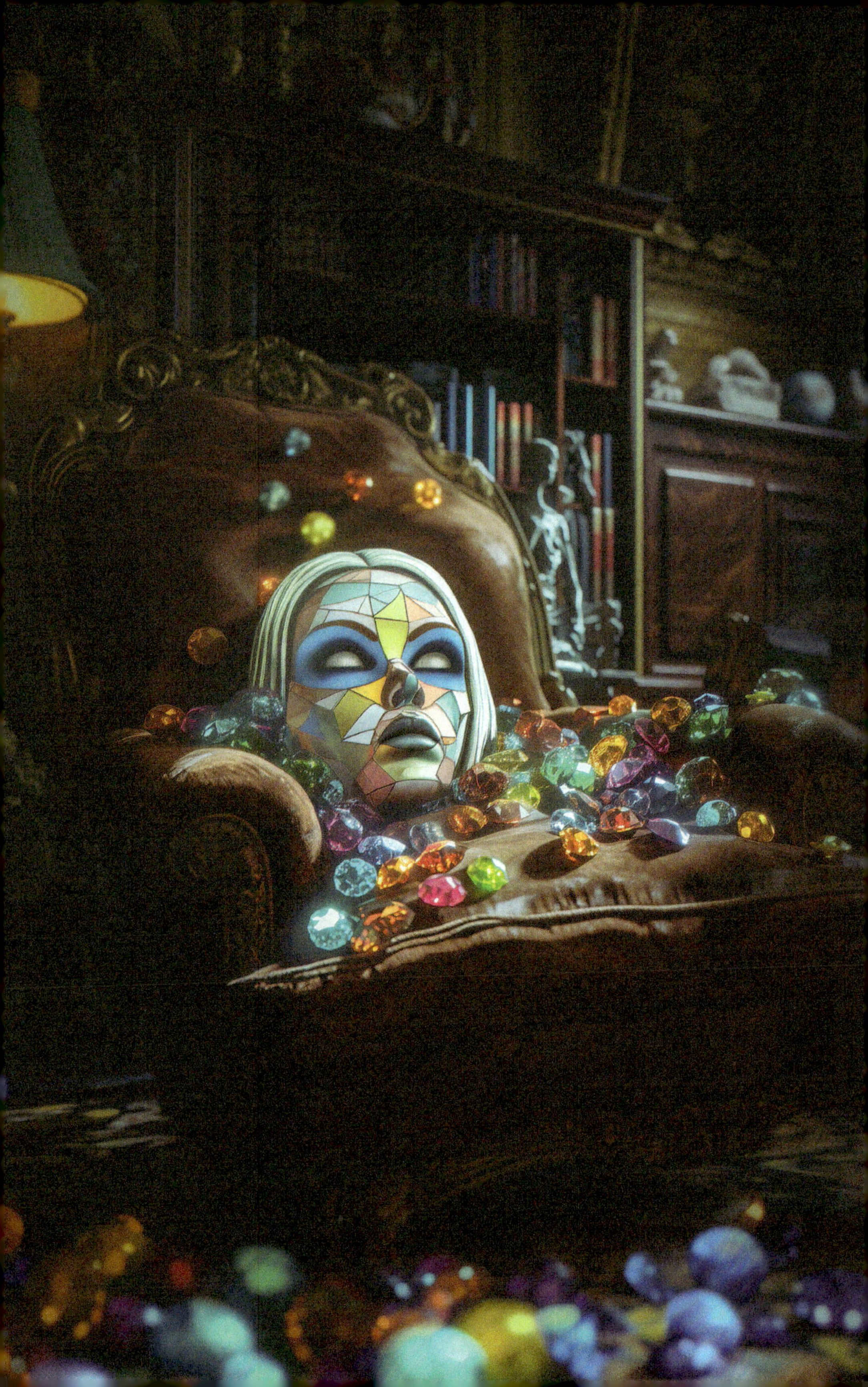

The patient finally freed herself from the puppet. To her surprise, the pain faded, and her hand relaxed. She laughed, almost tearfully, as she slowly removed the puppet, feeling lighter than she had in weeks.

Yet, as the puppet dropped from her fingers, her skin began to crack. She gasped, watching in horror as fissures of light snaked up her arm, spreading quickly across her body. Each breath deepened the cracks until her entire form fractured like glass.

In her final moment, she whispered, "It… it was holding me together…" Her body splintered, collapsing into a pile of glittering, multicolored gemstones, scattering across the office floor.

Dr. Wexler sits in his office, reminiscing about that day, haunted by the thought that his advice to free her led to her demise. Did he truly help her, or did he expedite her end?

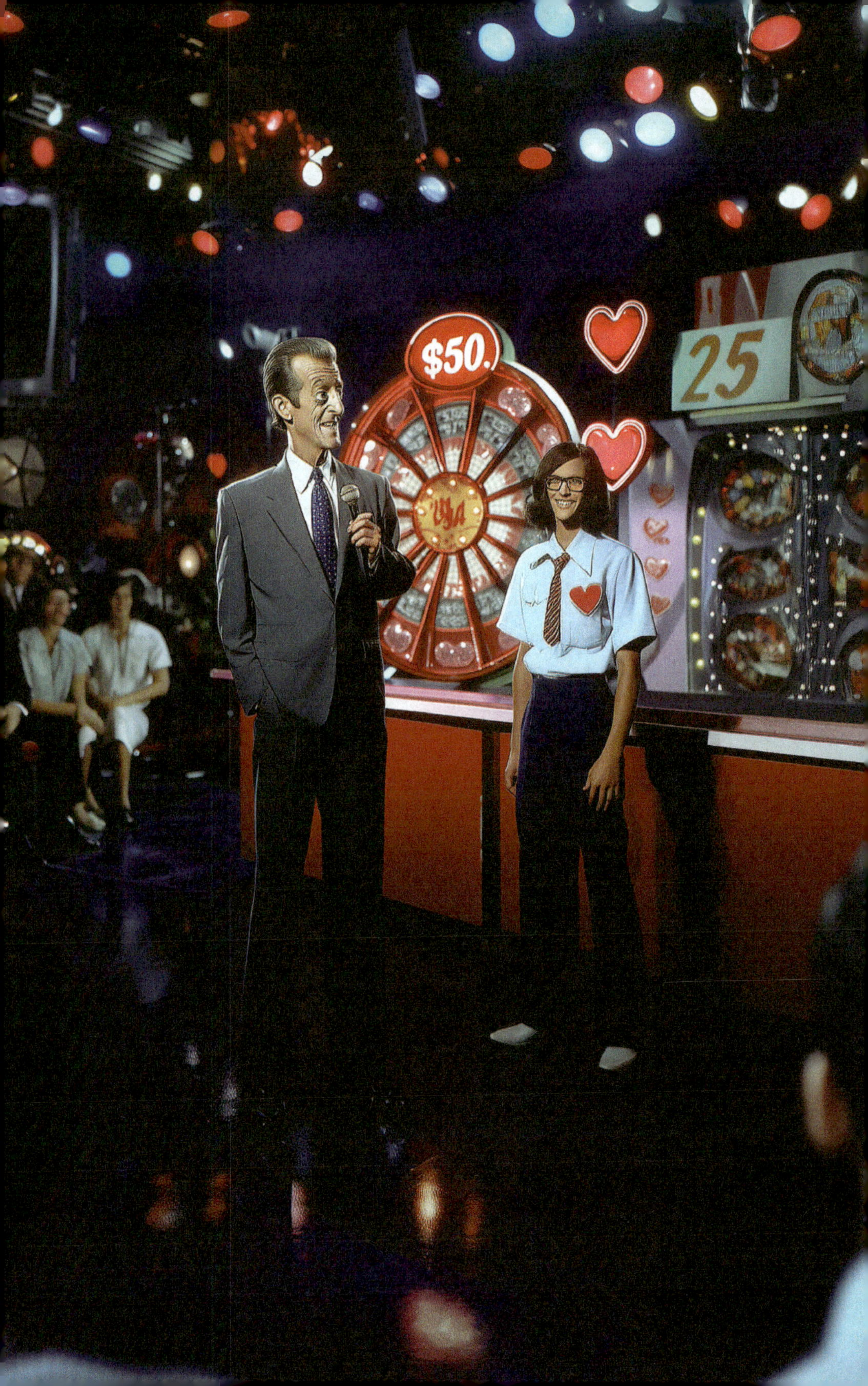
$50.
25

Dazzle Deal

You brushed dandruff off your shoulder as the Dazzle Deal jingle echoed through the studio. After hearing it countless times, it was hard to believe it was finally your turn. A crew member signaled that the cameras were rolling.

The famous host, David Darson, appeared, grinning. "Welcome, folks! Tonight, Martin is here to find love!" He explained the rules: meet a series of women, and at any point, you could settle down with the current contestant and take home the jackpot. Rejecting each woman would increase it, but if you reached the last contestant and agreed to marry her, you'd win double. You shivered, half-jokingly wondering what kind of woman they'd save for the finale.

David introduced you to the audience, then asked about your "type." He didn't seem to listen, but the audience roared as if you'd revealed a dark secret.

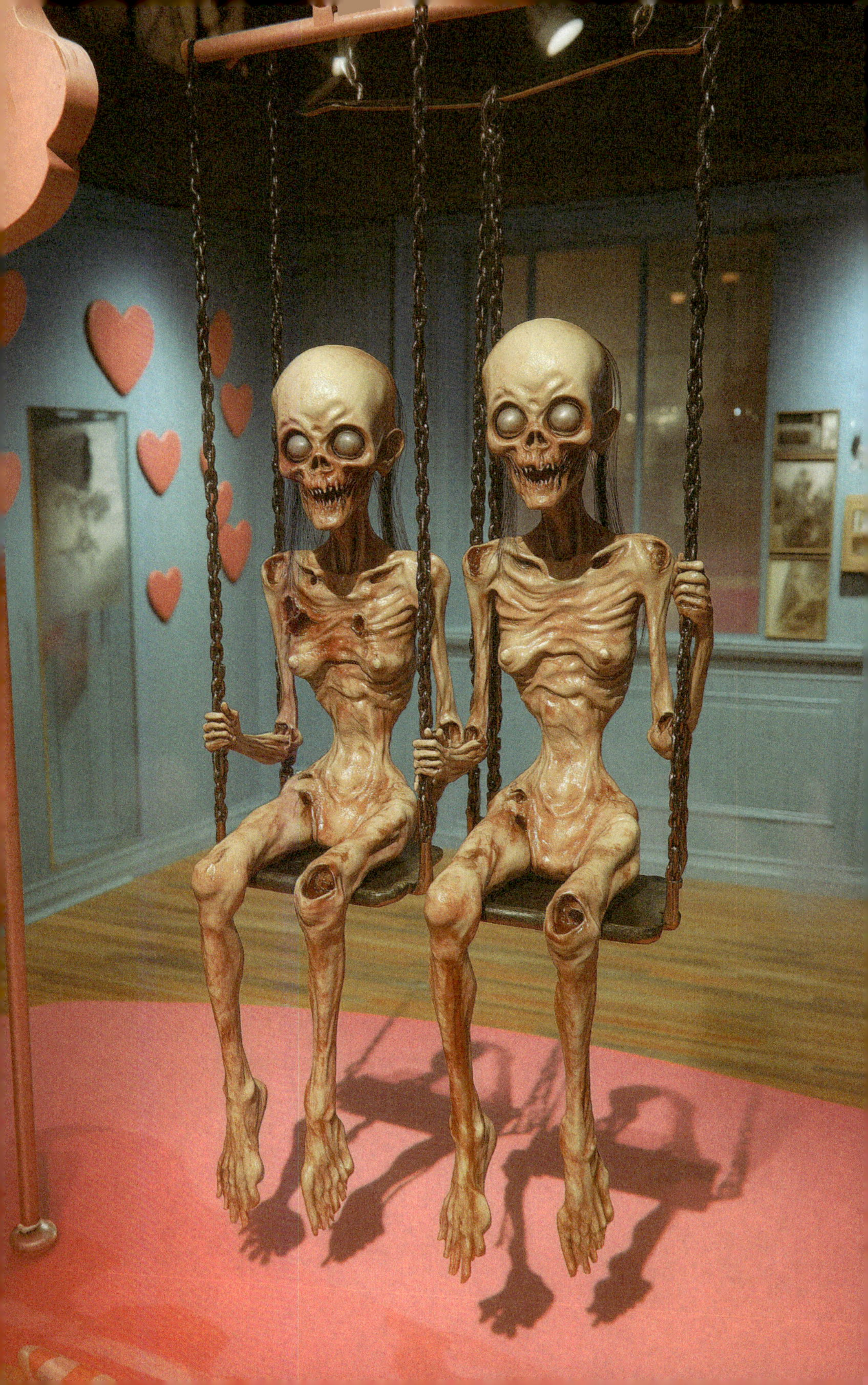

David handed you two darts, instructing you to aim for the largest jackpot. The crowd buzzed. You hit $20 on your first throw, and the audience erupted like it was a grand slam. An unseen voice described Bobby Sue, contestant one. You politely declined, and the audience cheered. David offered you the second dart.

You threw and hit $30. The crowd applauded. Sally, contestant two, was introduced. You hesitated, then rejected her too, and the audience cheered. David leaned in, hinting the "best" was yet to come, and the show cut to a commercial.

When the show returned, David explained the next round: Three doors, three women. Choose a door, meet the contestant, and decide whether to keep her or move on.

You chose door number 3. David beamed. "Let's see who's behind door three!" A slimy, gooey figure slid out, striking a distorted 1950s beauty-pageant pose. You recoiled as she gazed at you, winking. You turned to David, hoping for a laugh, but he just grinned and asked if you'd keep her or pass. You mumbled an apology, rejecting her. David slapped you on the back, chuckling about "real men making tough choices."

The next contestants were introduced with grand gestures: twins swinging on creaky swings. They looked disturbingly alike yet grotesquely wrong, like reflections in a funhouse mirror—one had an eye set too high, while the other's mouth twisted into a wide grin. Their limbs hung at odd angles as they swung, colliding in a strange rhythm. David teased that luck was on your side, but when you rejected them, they

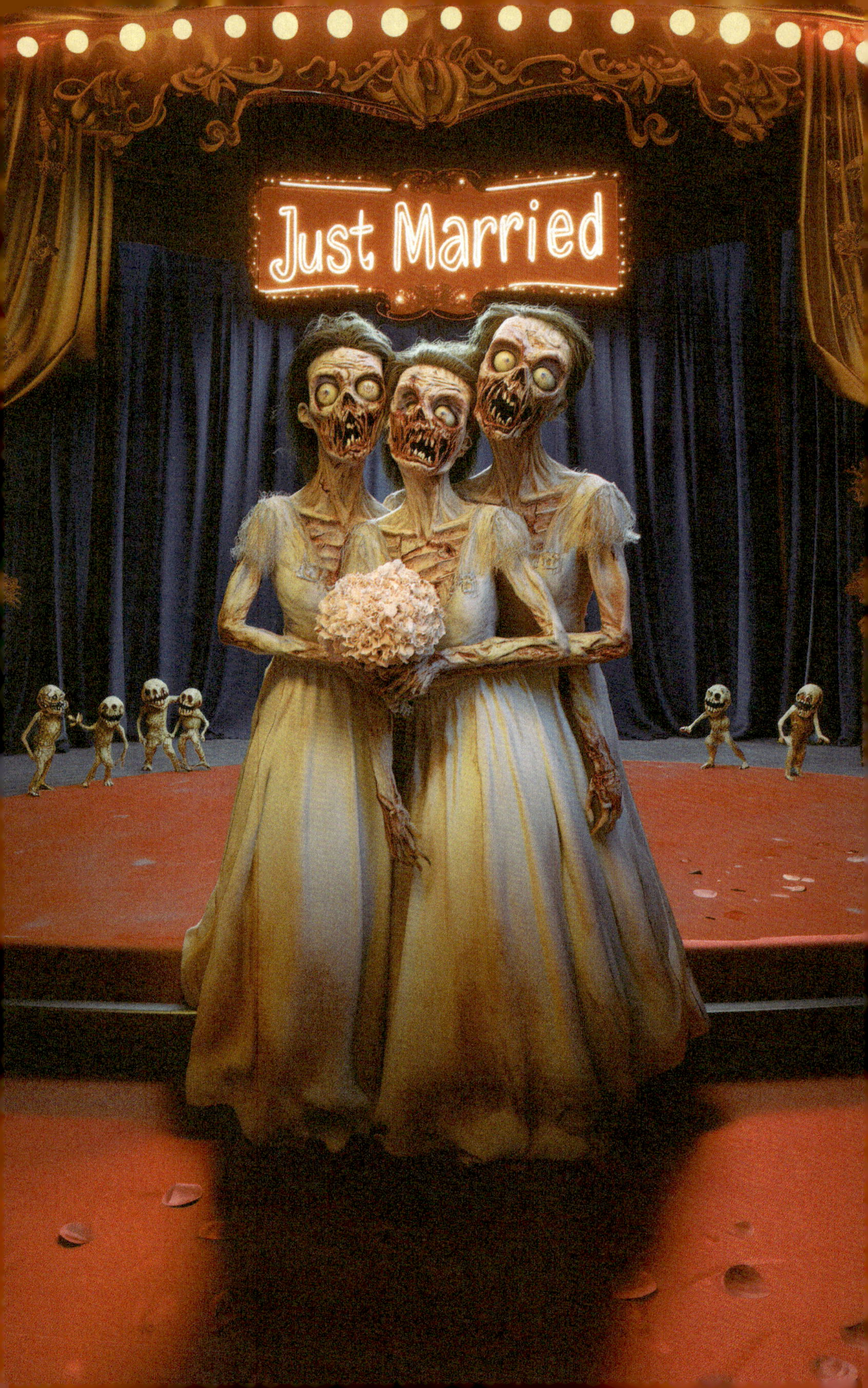
Just Married

wailed in eerie unison, blaming each other as they shuffled offstage, heads craning back toward you in disappointment.

Suddenly, a neon sign pulsed "SUDDEN DEATH." David's smile widened as two stagehands wheeled the set aside, revealing a blue curtain. "The stakes are high: you can leave empty-handed or marry the final contestant for the jackpot." Your mystery bride would only appear if you agreed. The crowd's strange gaze bore into you, the pulsing lights and drumroll blending in your head. Trembling, you agreed. Beauty is only skin-deep, you told yourself.

The curtain opened to a haunting tune as the final contestant emerged: conjoined triplets squeezed into a single, stretched wedding gown. Their twisted forms lurched forward, each head craning at you from uneven shoulders. Three pairs of mismatched eyes blinked in sync, their extra limbs twitching beneath the fabric as they shuffled down the catwalk, their fused bodies wearing a shared, toothy grin.

The audience erupted in applause, but you froze, paralyzed by this nightmare.

As the credits rolled and the jingle played, you glanced at the crowd and froze again. They weren't human at all. Shapeshifting beings, barely wearing human disguises, sat in silent applause. The realization hit you like a chill: you'd been the only human here all along—the only candidate.

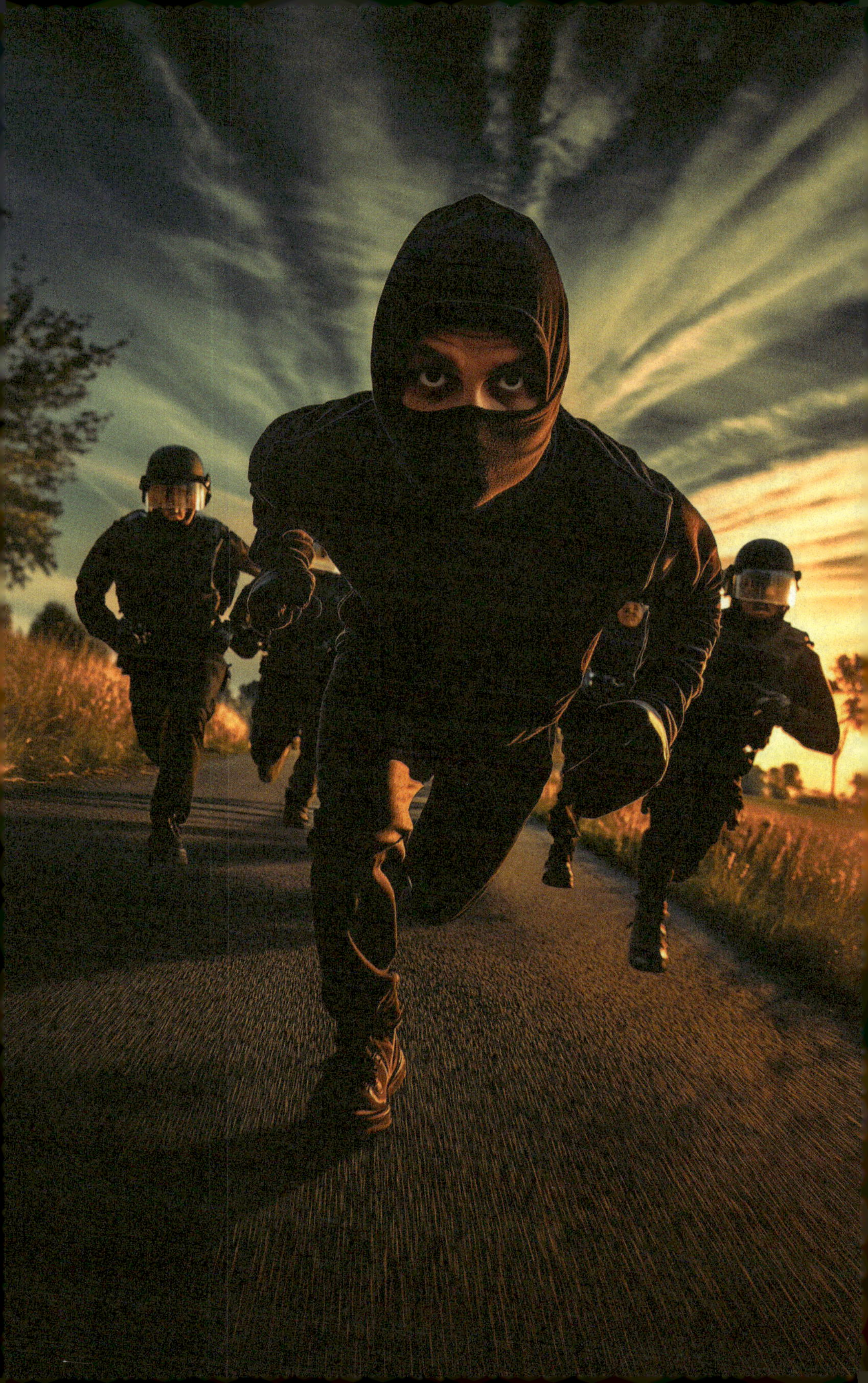

Celestial Escape

Chased by four policemen, Will, hooded and masked, sprinted through the fields toward a distant carnival in the countryside. In the sky, a few hot air balloons drifted slowly. When he arrived, he noticed that only one balloon remained on the ground, and he decided that this would be his escape.

As Will entered the carnival, he was taken aback to find the place eerily quiet and abandoned. The rides, once full of laughter and excitement, now stood silent and rusting. He quickly searched for a place to hide, but the sounds of the approaching police were too close for comfort. They would see him if he tried to conceal himself in the shadows. Just when he thought he was out of options, he spotted it: the last hot air balloon, still tethered to the ground.

The balloon operator, seemingly oblivious to Will's desperation, cheerfully offered him a ride for just one dollar. Will felt a surge of frustration; he didn't have a penny to his name. In a moment of panic, he brandished his gun, threatening the

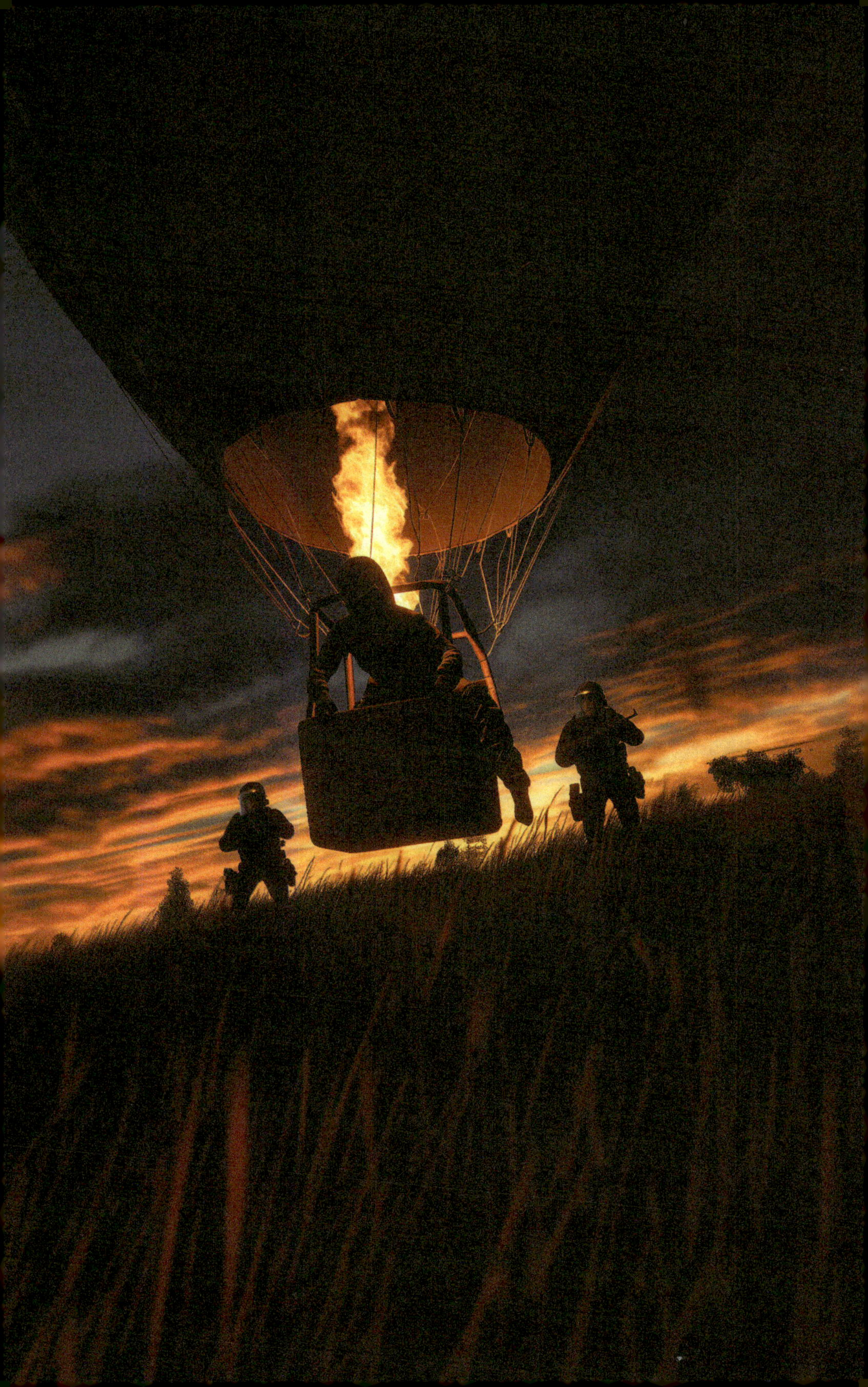

operator and forcing him out of the basket. Climbing in, Will asked the operator how to operate the burner. "You'll figure it out," the operator said, shrugging. "This thing basically flies itself."

Just as Will began to ascend, gunfire erupted behind him. The cops shot at the balloon, and he could hear bullets whizzing past as they pierced through the fabric. Surprisingly, the balloon didn't deflate. Instead, it continued to rise higher and higher. Will couldn't help but laugh in disbelief; it was as if the balloon had a mind of its own. He soared into the sky, soon disappearing among the clouds.

For a few moments, Will savored his unexpected victory. The thrill of escape flooded his senses, but that joy was short-lived. Suddenly, he heard a voice coming from above. "We're almost there!" At first, he was startled, unsure of where the voice was coming from. But then, with growing horror, he realized the voice was coming from the balloon itself.

"Wait, what?" Will exclaimed, feeling a mix of surprise and dread. He asked the balloon to take him back down, but it simply replied, "I want to reach the sun. It won't be long now."

Panic surged through him as he stopped the burner, hoping to halt the ascent. But instead of descending, the balloon only complained about the cold. Frantically, Will began shooting at the balloon, emptying his gun in a desperate attempt to escape. To his dismay, nothing worked; the balloon continued its ascent, undeterred by his efforts.

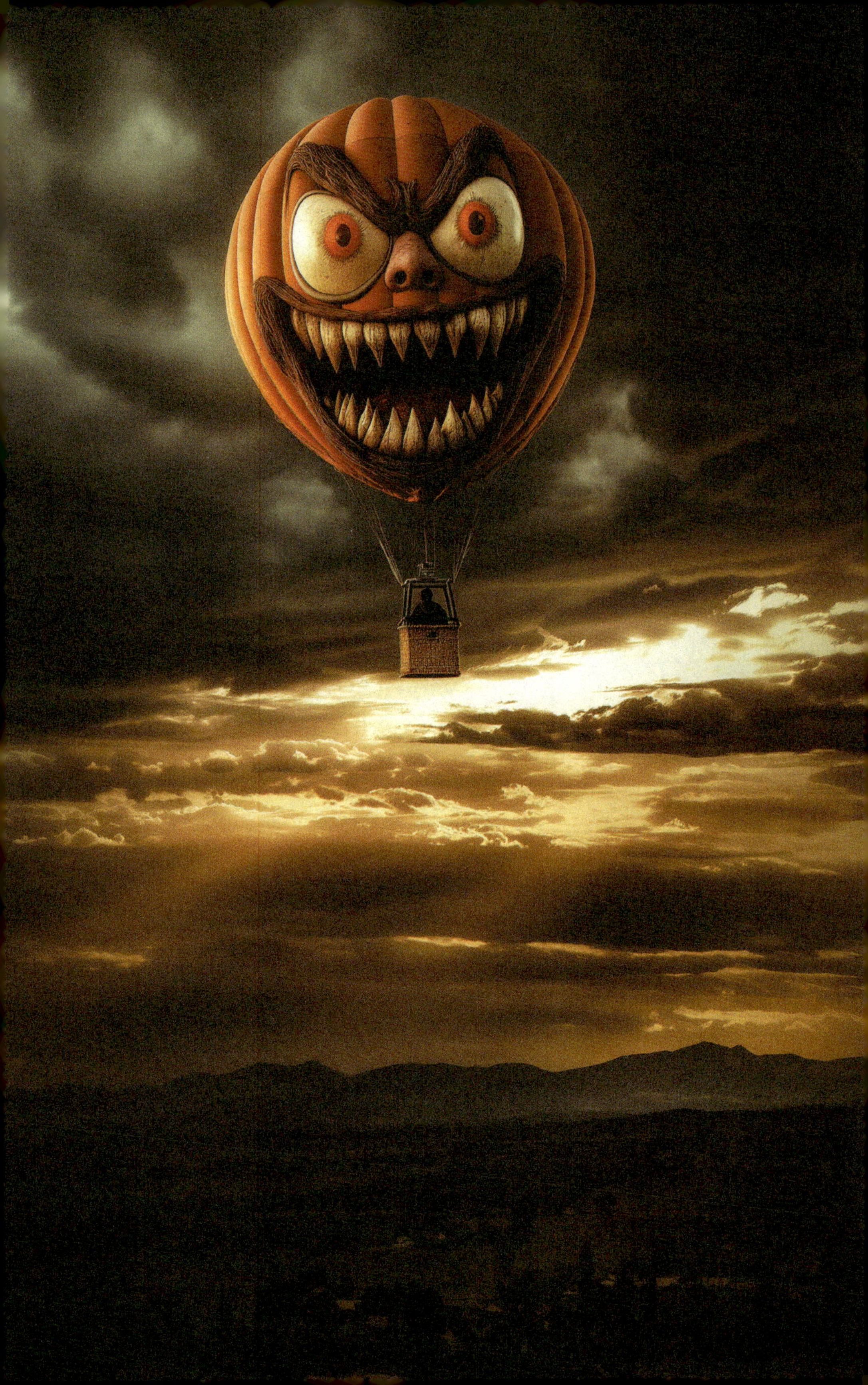

Will considered jumping out, but the thought of plummeting to the ground was terrifying. He looked up, realizing that the sun was getting closer and closer, its heat intensifying around him. Dehydration began to take its toll, and as he rose toward the sky, he felt the suffocating grip of fear mixed with an overwhelming thirst. The realization hit him hard: he was trapped, forever bound to the whims of a balloon that only wanted to fly to the sun.

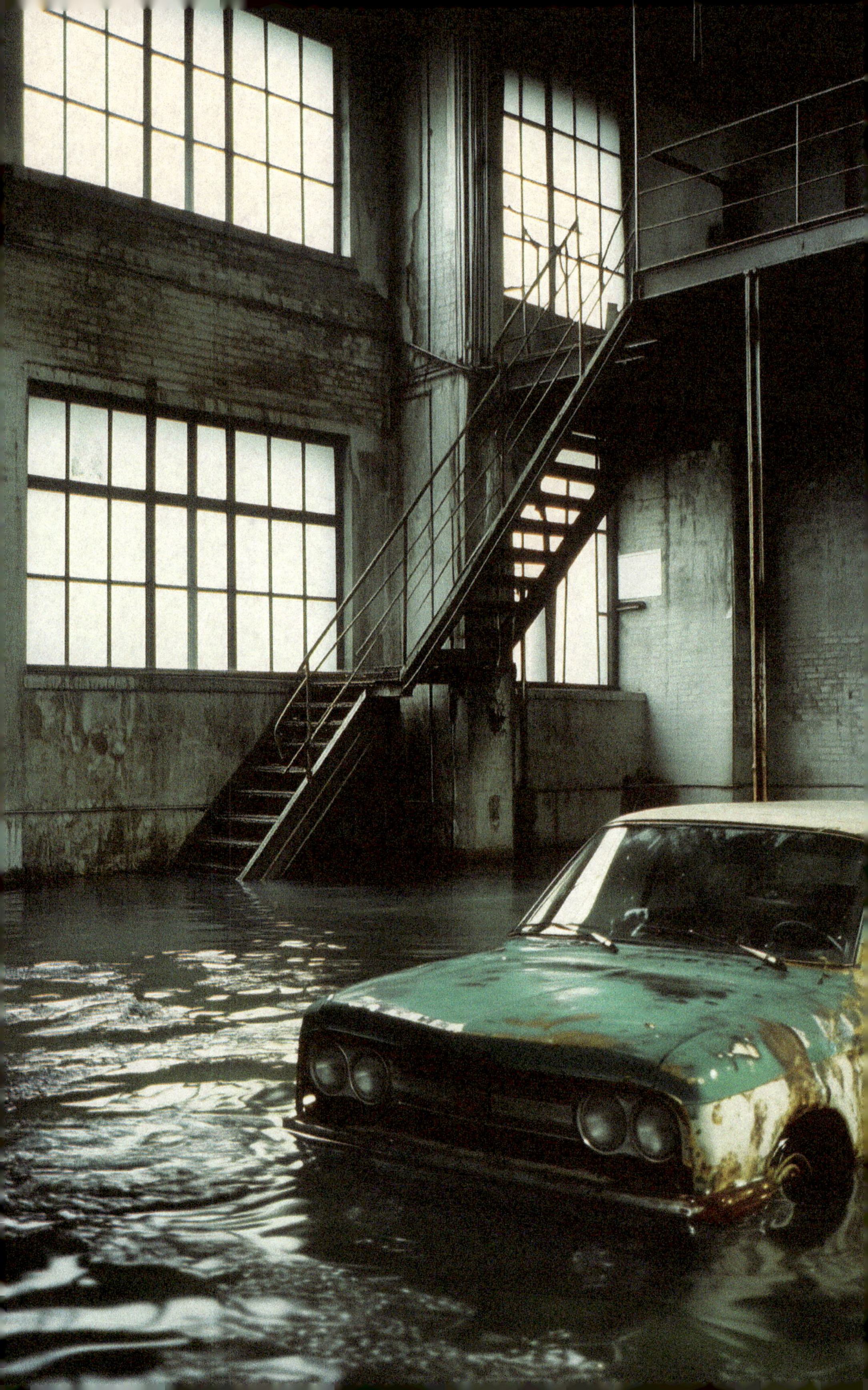

Aquatic Fascination

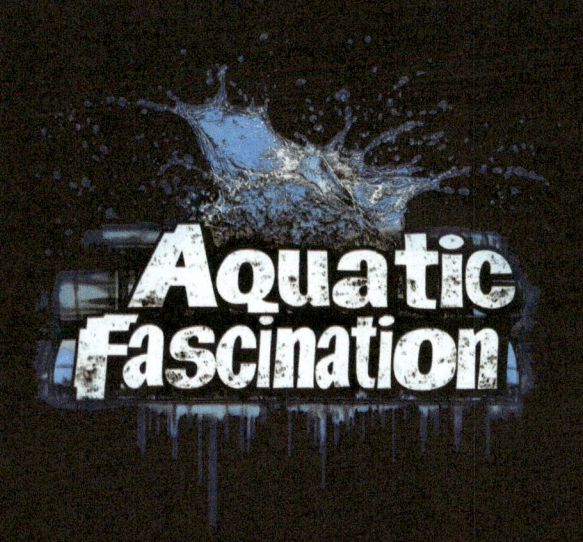

The voices had led Vincent to the crumbling apartment building. They whispered urgently, reminding him that his goddess needed him, urging him to lift her to the top of the tower.

Dressed in a tattered sailor outfit, he stepped into the lobby and activated the sprinklers. Water burst forth, flooding the entrance in a chaotic torrent. His mind raced, consumed by the belief that he was meant to summon his goddess. In a fevered haze, he descended into the basement, smashing pipes with frantic determination. Water pooled around him, reflecting the chaos inside his head.

He imagined himself swimming toward freedom, fear gripping him as he worried about drowning if he didn't move quickly enough. Desperation fueled him as Vincent burst through the flooded hallway and climbed the stairs, the water lapping at his ankles. On the second floor, he turned on all the faucets, letting them gush uncontrollably. Each sound

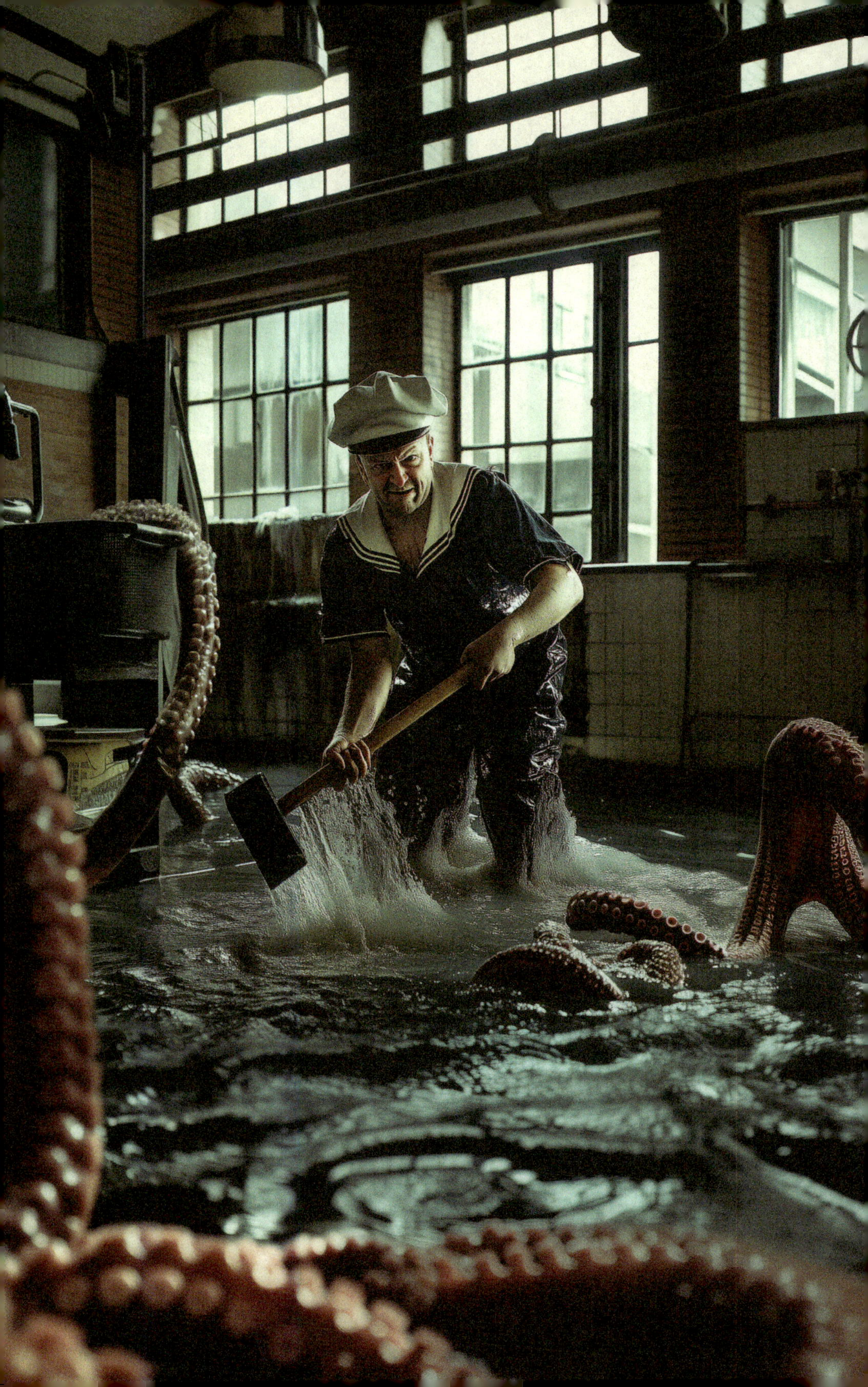

echoed like the voices in his mind, growing louder and more insistent as he felt himself teetering on the edge of madness.

In the janitor's area, he finally found his goddess: a monstrous figure lurking in the shadows. She loomed large, an imagined octopus, her tentacles reaching toward him. The creature spoke in a voice that resonated deep within him, promising salvation if he helped raise her to a higher floor. With renewed purpose, Vincent sprinted through the flooded third floor, adrenaline coursing through him as the water threatened to swallow him whole.

He broke into an apartment, shattering kitchen pipes with wild abandon. Water gushed out, a chaotic symphony reflecting his unraveling sanity. Climbing more stairs, each step felt heavier, each breath a struggle against the rising deluge.

Then came a moment of dread. As he jumped to avoid a tentacle that flicked dangerously close, fear gripped his heart. For a fleeting second, he questioned his devotion to her. Was she truly benevolent, or was she dragging him deeper into madness? But there was no turning back; he was almost at the top floor, and the water continued to rise, an ever-present threat.

He finally spotted the hallway leading to the roof and raced toward it. His heart pounded as he sprinted for the elevator, slamming the doors shut just as the water surged in, desperate to claim him.

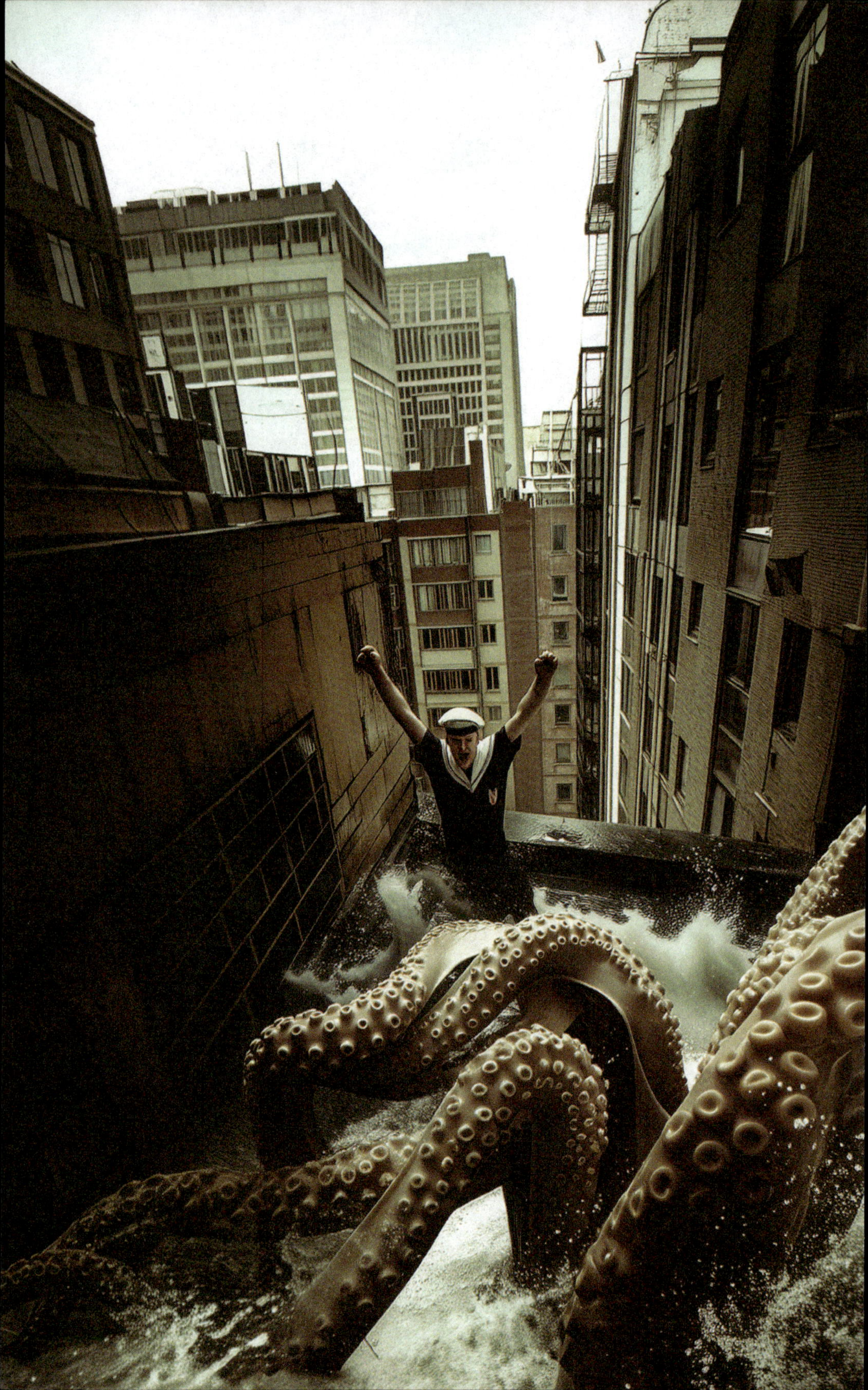

With one last push, he reached the roof, gasping for air, a wave of relief washing over him. He had succeeded. He had pleased his goddess. On the roof, she awaited him, presenting the promised vial of vitalium—a beautiful crystal flask filled with a blue potion.

Vincent clutched the vial tightly, a glimmering promise of healing. Deep down, he knew that this potion would mend his fractured mind and silence the visions, but it would also erase his goddess if she was merely a hallucination. The truth loomed large in his mind: he had done all of this for a gift that could save him or doom him to a life without her.

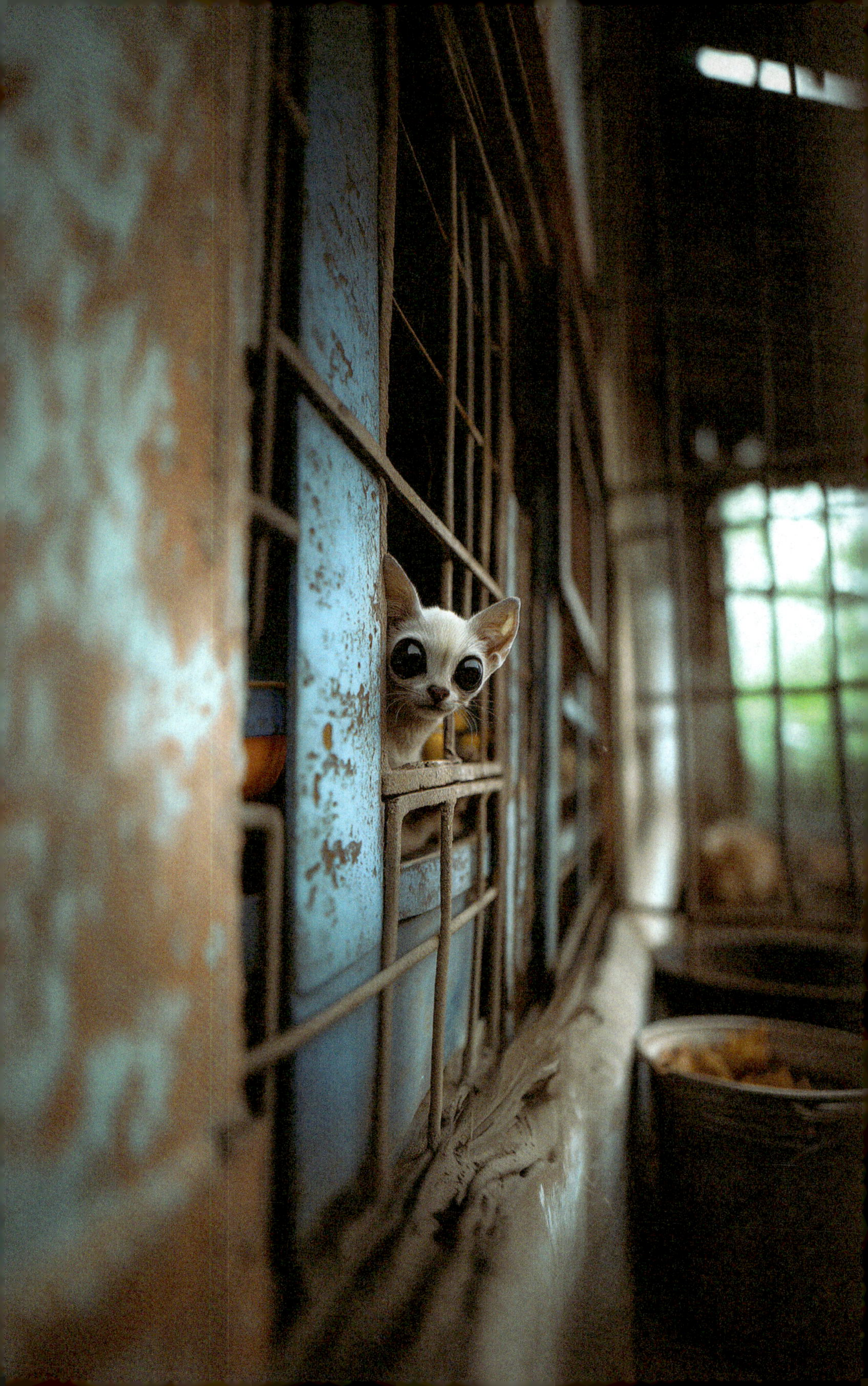

Cat Dog

Brian hadn't planned to stray, but the draw of a new woman he'd met online had pulled him in. She was quiet but intense, with a fierce sense of justice—especially about animal rights. After they shared bubble tea, she insisted on stopping by a nearby animal shelter. She called it a cruel place, where animals suffered while the shelter profited.

Inside, the smell was overpowering, the air thick with the stench of neglected animals. There were cages everywhere, some so flimsy it seemed the animals could break free at any moment. That's when Brian noticed an odd creature, tucked away in a rusty cage. It looked like a strange mix of cat and dog, small and skittish, with curious eyes. His date grew furious at the sight, and without hesitation, she began opening cages, urging the animals to flee. She handed the strange creature to Brian and told him to run. Against his better judgment, he did.

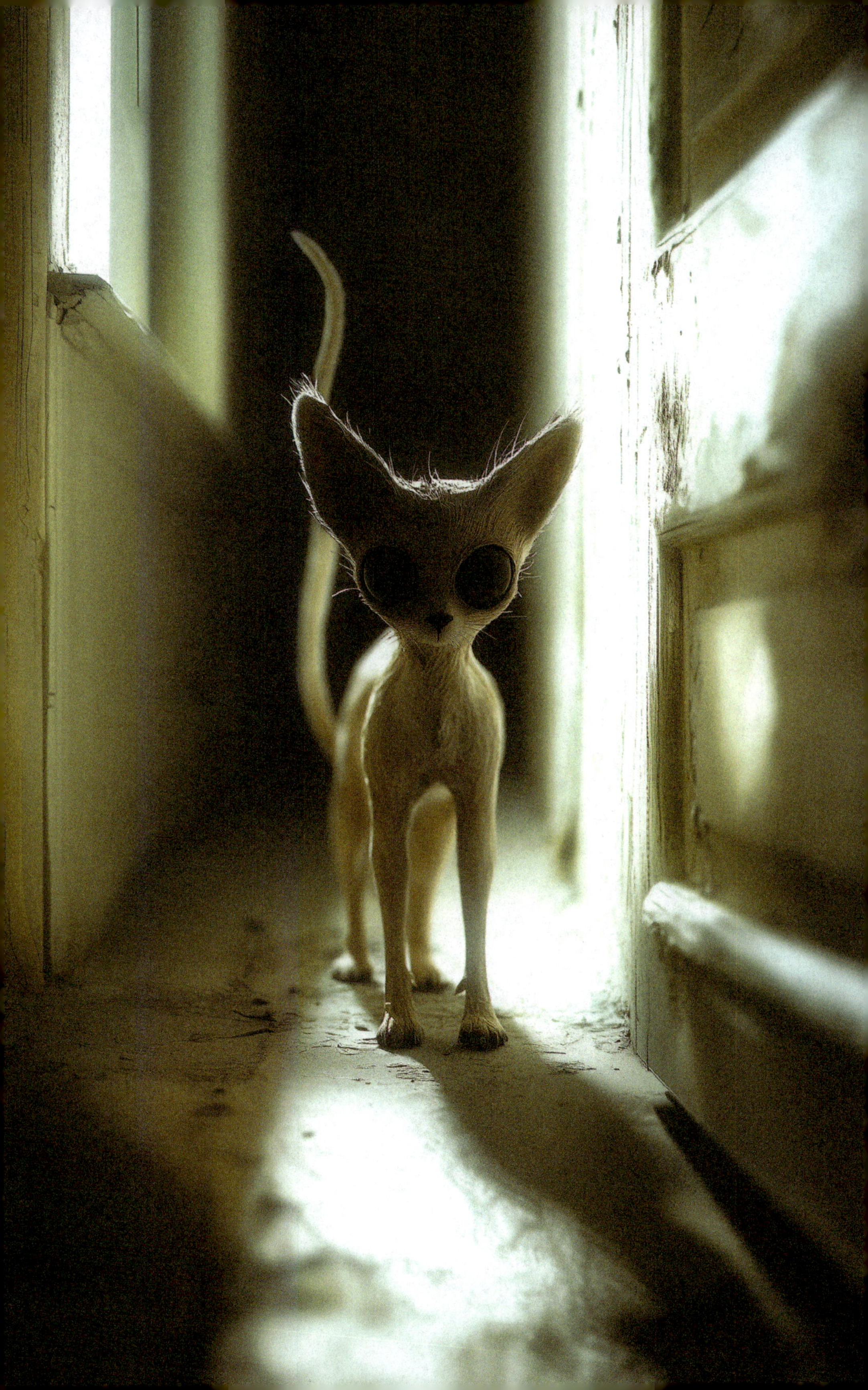

Later, she convinced him to keep the animal, calling it "Catdog." Brian wasn't sure why, but something about it intrigued him. Besides, he'd been thinking about getting a pet. The small creature was oddly endearing, though his girlfriend had once scoffed that he could barely take care of himself, let alone a pet.

A week later, Brian left town for a weekend with his girlfriend, thinking the time away might calm her suspicions. He left food, water, and a litter box for Catdog, confident it would be enough. He even left the TV on for company.

When he returned, though, his apartment was a wreck. Holes marred the walls, the smell of urine was suffocating, and the TV screen had a massive dent. Then, to his horror, he saw Catdog—but it had changed. It was now the size of a human, wearing one of Brian's grimy garage jumpsuits and glaring at him with familiar eyes.

"Catdogs don't watch TV, Brian," it sneered, speaking in Brian's own voice. "Catdogs need attention, or else we break things."

Brian froze, feeling cold all over as he tried to understand what he was seeing. The sight made his stomach turn. Catdog's eyes locked onto him with an intense, almost angry focus, as if it recognized him in a way no animal ever should. Its stare was fixed, unblinking, and filled with something unsettlingly close to human anger. It started to pace back and forth, each step awkward and stiff, almost like it was

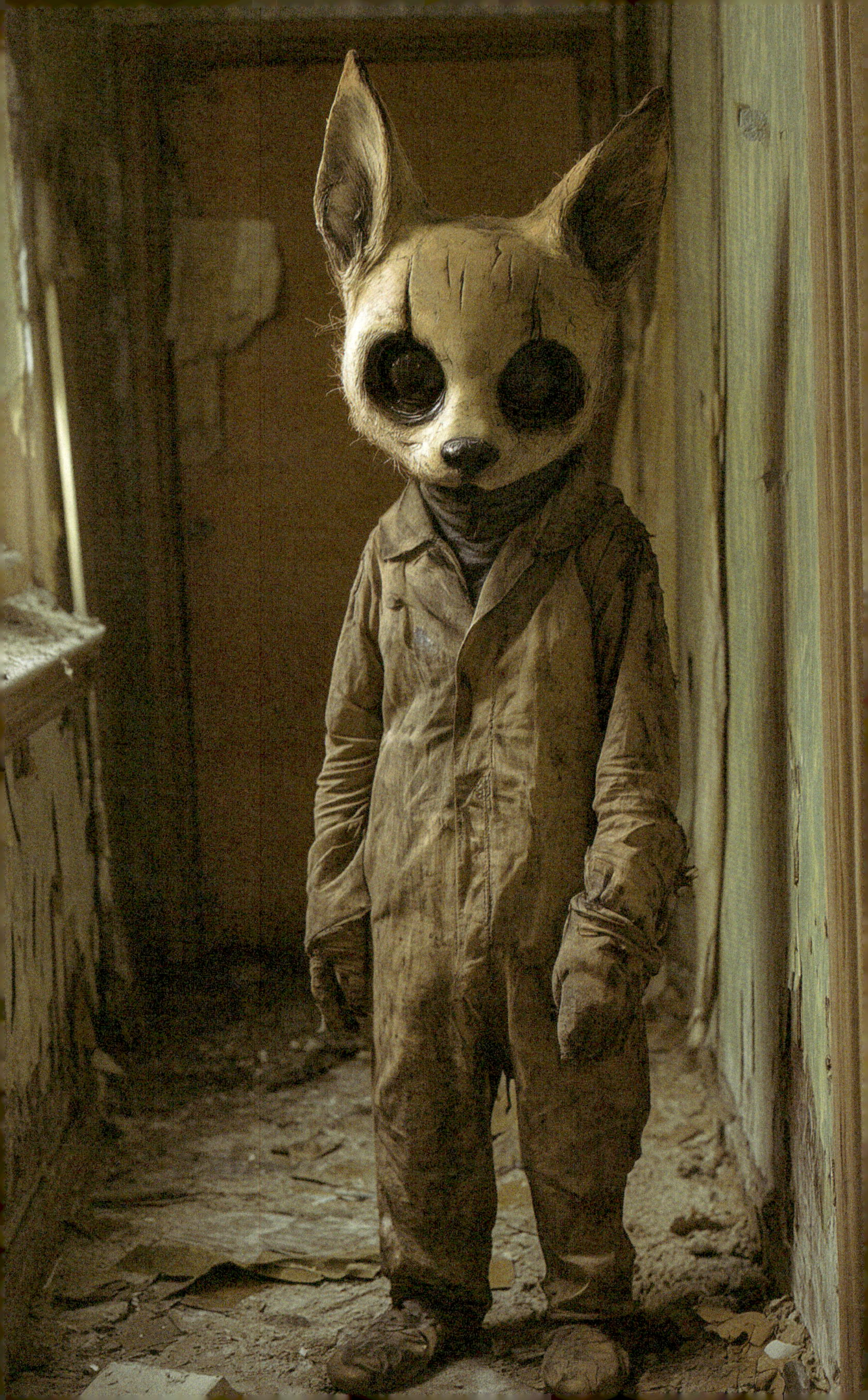

forcing itself to move like a person. The whole time, its eyes never left Brian.

Then it spoke, using a voice that sounded disturbingly like Brian's own, but warped and wrong. It explained, in that strange, flat tone, that it could copy anything it saw. At the shelter, it had copied cats and dogs, but here, alone in the apartment, it had been watching him. It had picked up on all his routines, his habits, even his voice. It knew things about him now—everything he'd done, everything he'd tried to hide. And now it stood there, mimicking him perfectly, a twisted version of himself staring back at him.

Catdog started listing Brian's secrets, things he thought only he knew: the dating sites he used, his excuses to his girlfriend, the lies he told himself. It spoke of these things calmly, yet with a tone that made Brian's skin crawl. His secret life was no longer a secret.

"You're going to keep me fed," Catdog declared, its eyes narrowing. "You're going to keep my litterbox clean. And I'll be staying in your bedroom from now on. You can use the couch."

Brian tried to argue, but Catdog's stare stopped him cold. It was clear there would be no escaping this creature. And as it leaned closer, it added one last warning, its voice low and chilling: "Leave me alone again, Brian, and you won't like what happens."

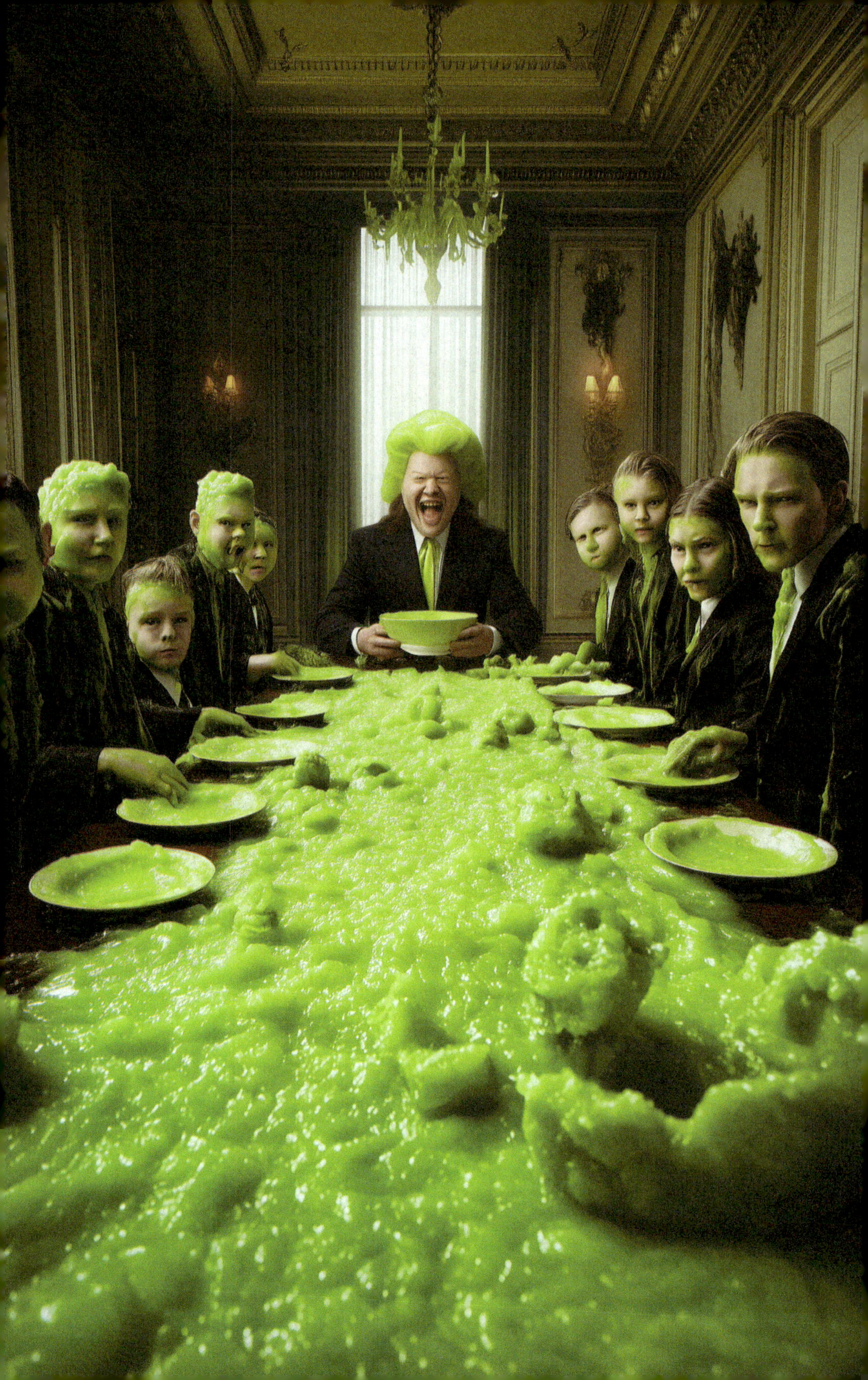

Jelly Feast

Lewis adjusted his tie, glancing up at the massive, looming estate. His girlfriend had mentioned her family was "a little quirky," but this was more than he'd expected—huge staircases, walls covered with old paintings, chandeliers casting dim, yellow light. He took a steadying breath and stepped inside.

Right away, he noticed a strange whistling sound drifting down the hall, growing louder as he entered the dining room. Her whole family was seated around a grand table, all focused on bowls of bright lime-green jelly. But they weren't just eating it—they were covered in it. Her brother had it smeared across his cheeks, her mother's hands were shiny with the stuff, and they hummed a strange, off-key tune as they ate, whistling in a trance-like harmony. His girlfriend beamed, her lips stained faintly green, and handed him a bowl of his own. "Just try a little," she said, her eyes glassy.

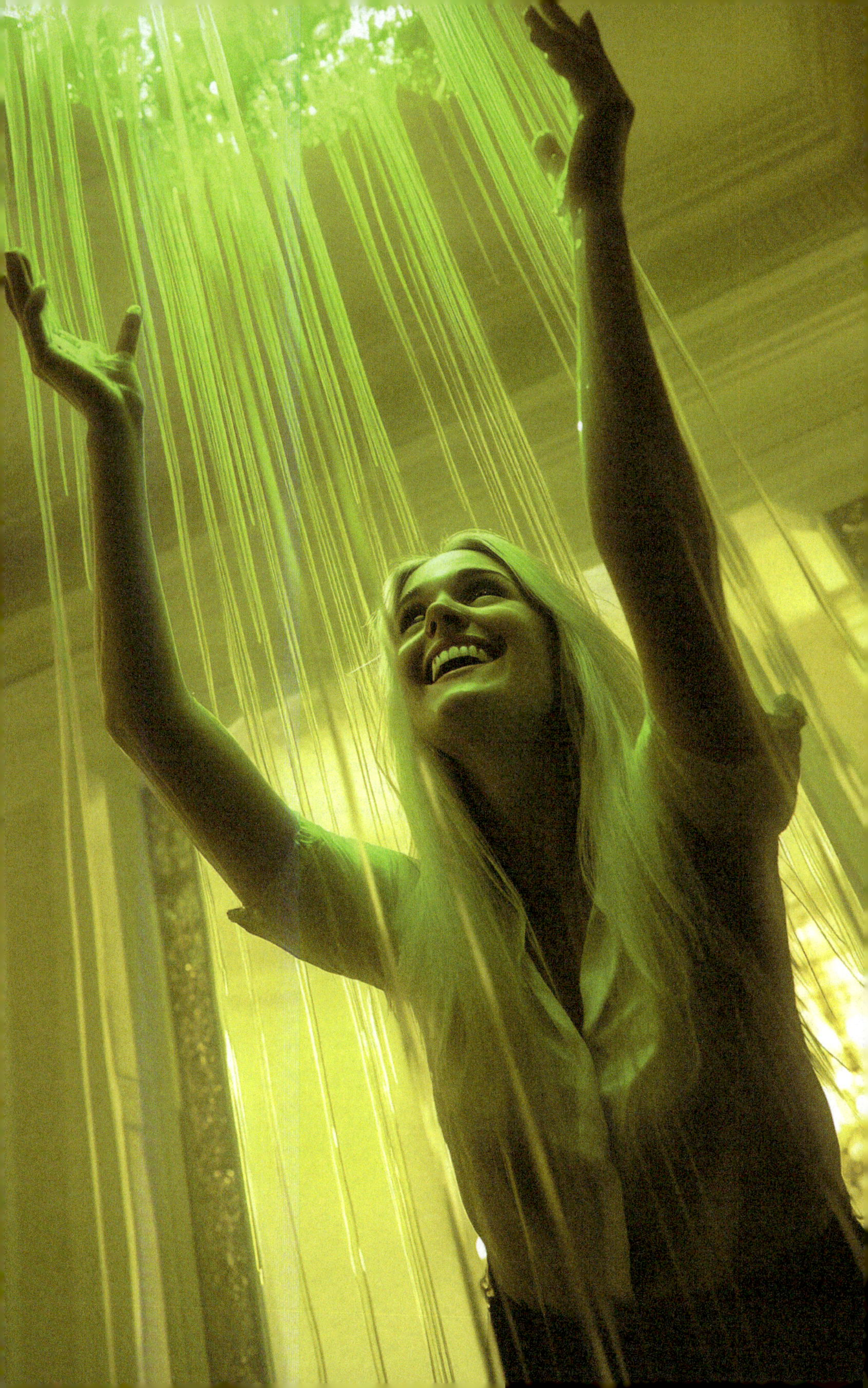

Lewis hesitated, staring at the bowl of jelly. Its sickly-sweet, metallic smell made his stomach turn, but not wanting to seem rude, he lifted a spoonful to his mouth. Just as it touched his lips, he stopped, letting the jelly fall back into the bowl when no one was looking. He forced a smile, wiping his mouth to keep up the act.

"Attaboy!" Her father clapped him on the back, grinning in a way that made Lewis nervous. "Now you're one of us!" The father's eyes glinted, and Lewis chuckled, hoping for reassurance from his girlfriend. But she was completely focused on her own bowl, spooning up the jelly with an empty, dazed look.

He tried to fake another bite, but her younger brother caught him. "Saw you spit it out," he muttered, staring suspiciously. The table fell silent, and the family all turned to look at him, their eyes cold.

"What's wrong?" her father asked. "You haven't touched your plate."

Lewis stammered, the strange taste still lingering on his tongue. "I… just need a moment," he mumbled, turning to his girlfriend. "Bathroom?" She nodded, giggling, and stood up, unfazed by the tension in the room. She led him down a dim hallway, moving with a loose, drifting walk, as if she was floating. The walls had a faint greenish glow, a sheen of something slimy coating the wallpaper, and he felt a strange heaviness settle over him.

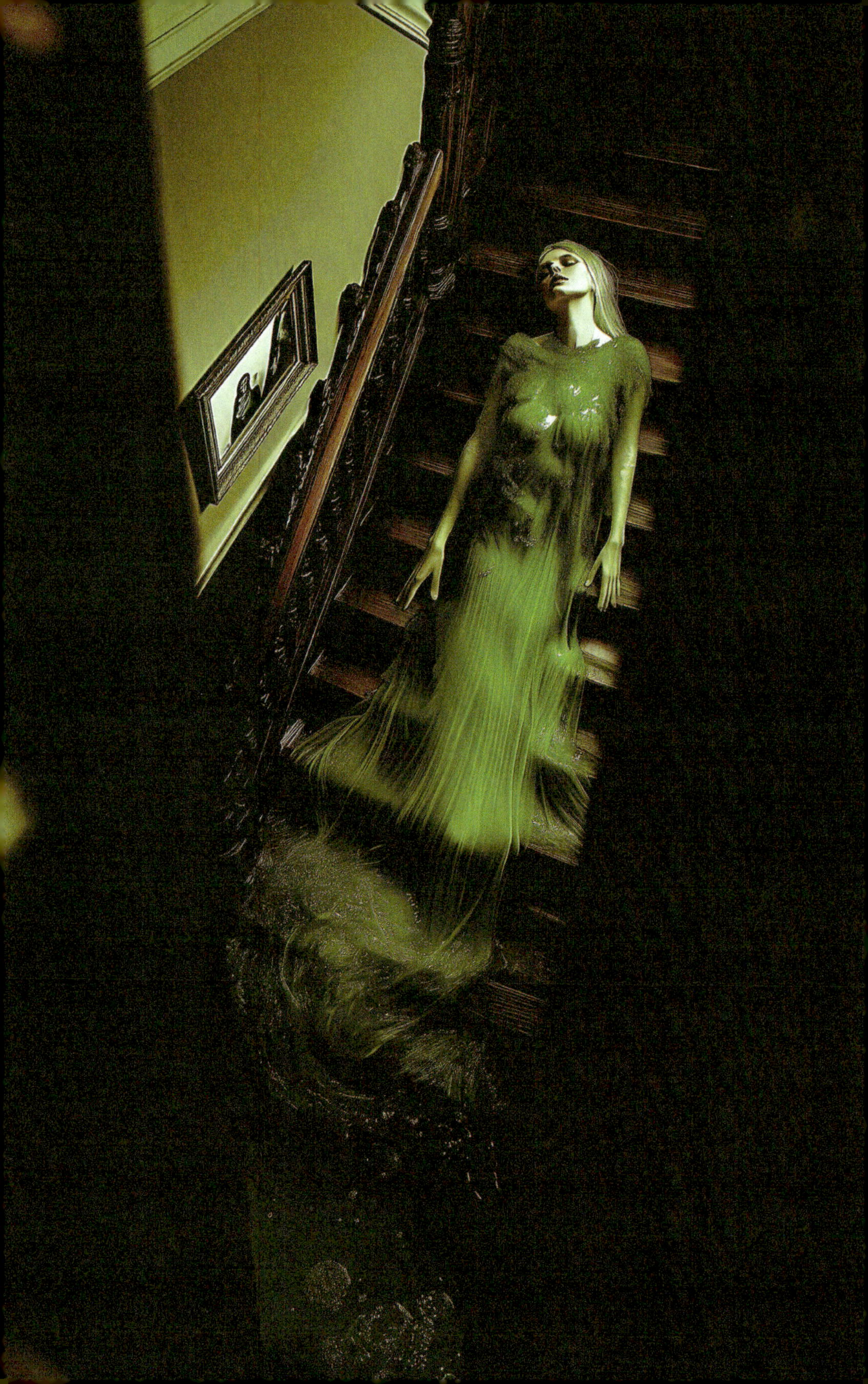

She paused, leaning close, her face dreamy, her breath thick and sweet. "You feel it, don't you?" she whispered. "The call?"

Before he could answer, she turned away, swaying as she moved back toward the grand staircase. Her hands trailed along the walls, leaving faint green streaks. She hummed softly, dancing lightly as if to a song only she could hear, her eyes unfocused.

At the top of the stairs, she took a step forward without looking. Her foot slipped, and she fell, her body hitting each step with a sickening, wet sound, leaving streaks of green behind her. With each impact, her form seemed to soften, dissolving bit by bit, until she landed at the bottom in a gleaming pool of green slime, still faintly shimmering.

Lewis stood frozen, his mind blank. His hand drifted into his pocket, where he found another jelly ball. Almost without thinking, he lifted it to his mouth, the metallic sweetness filling his senses. His pulse slowed, his thoughts softened, and a strange tune bubbled up in his throat.

He began to whistle.

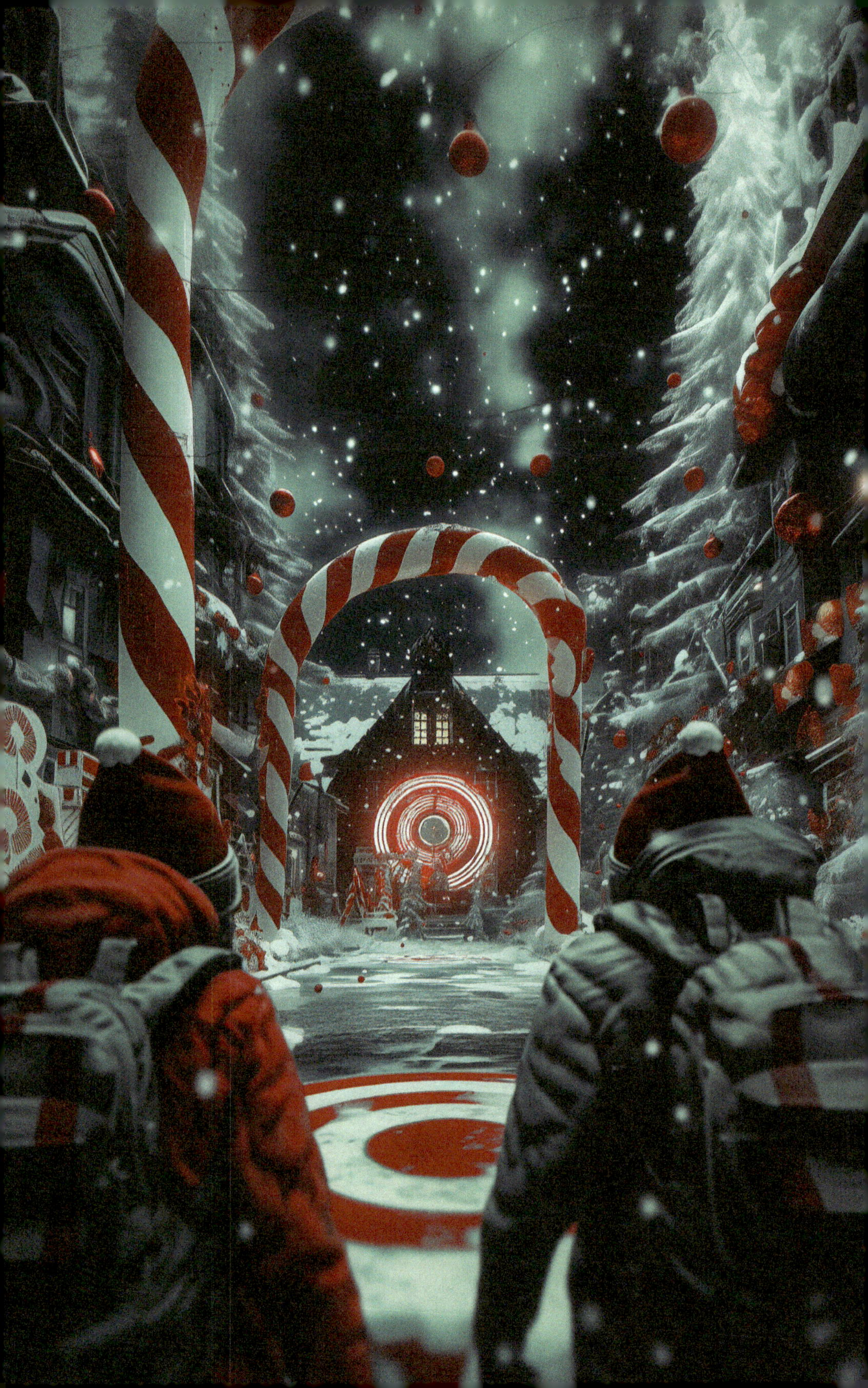

Santa Hell

Ethan and Jake had been hiding in the mall bathroom for half an hour, passing a cheap bottle of booze and waiting for the place to close. It was three days before Christmas, and they had one plan: cause some chaos in Santa's Village. Ethan laughed, remembering how he'd always looked too old for Santa's lap as a kid. Jake muttered that mall Santas were creepy anyway, claiming he'd seen this one before and that the guy reeked of candy canes.

When the mall finally fell silent, they slipped out, heading for Santa's Village. The dim lights made the decorations look eerie, shadows stretching from the big plastic trees. Jake blasted a heavy metal Christmas song from his phone, the sound echoing through the empty space. He tried to jump a picket fence but toppled it instead, the whole row collapsing in a loud clatter. Smirking, Ethan sprayed a sloppy, drunken "Happy Hell Days." Jake laughed, but the laughter cut short when a snowflake drifted down from above. Ethan reached

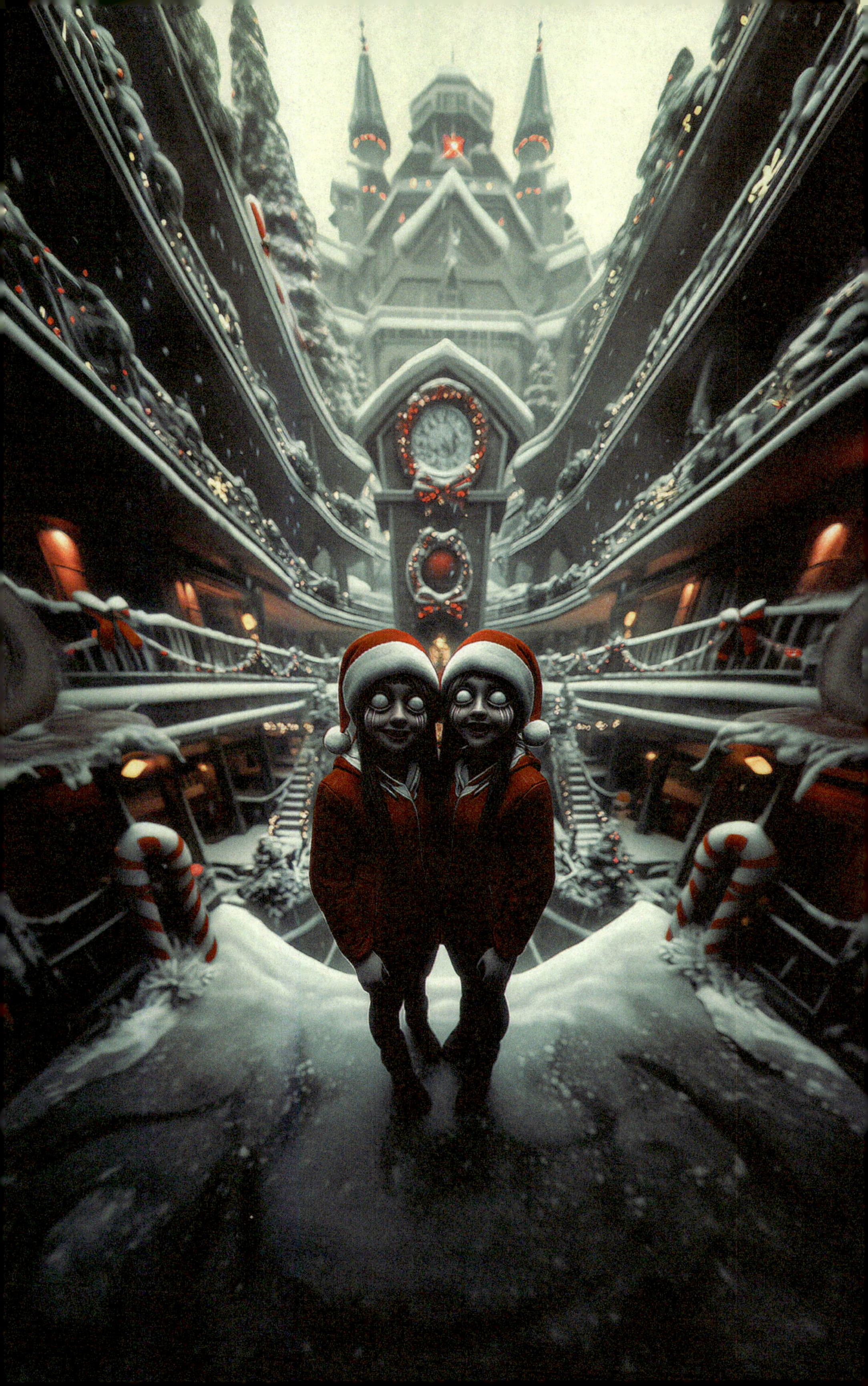

out to touch it, shivering as the air around them grew cold, impossibly fast.

Suddenly, a swirling portal appeared before them, its surface shifting and twisting. Both boys froze, eyes wide. The portal expanded, and a small figure tumbled out—a wide-eyed, grinning elf who moved in jerky, unnatural motions. She cocked her head, staring, before inviting them to step through, promising they'd find proof that Santa was real. Jake snickered, but the elf's eerie laughter joined his, echoing through the darkened mall.

Inside, the world twisted around them, like a haunted version of the mall mixed with a nightmarish Christmas village. The elf left them with three strange rules: head north, don't talk to strangers, and never eat the dandy canes. They shrugged it off, guessing north might be toward a glowing symbol in the distance—concentric circles carved into a stone wall.

As they walked, they reached a maze twisting into the shadows. The alcohol was wearing off, and each turn seemed darker and colder. Both of them stumbled, nearly slipping on patches of ice. At last, they emerged, only to find themselves surrounded by candy canes of all sizes, planted like sinister decorations. Jake grabbed one and shrugged, laughing nervously. "Might as well get a snack," he muttered. Ethan hesitated but took a bite too, ignoring the elf's warning.

Almost immediately, they felt an intense sugar rush, an electric energy buzzing under their skin. A dizzy warmth spread

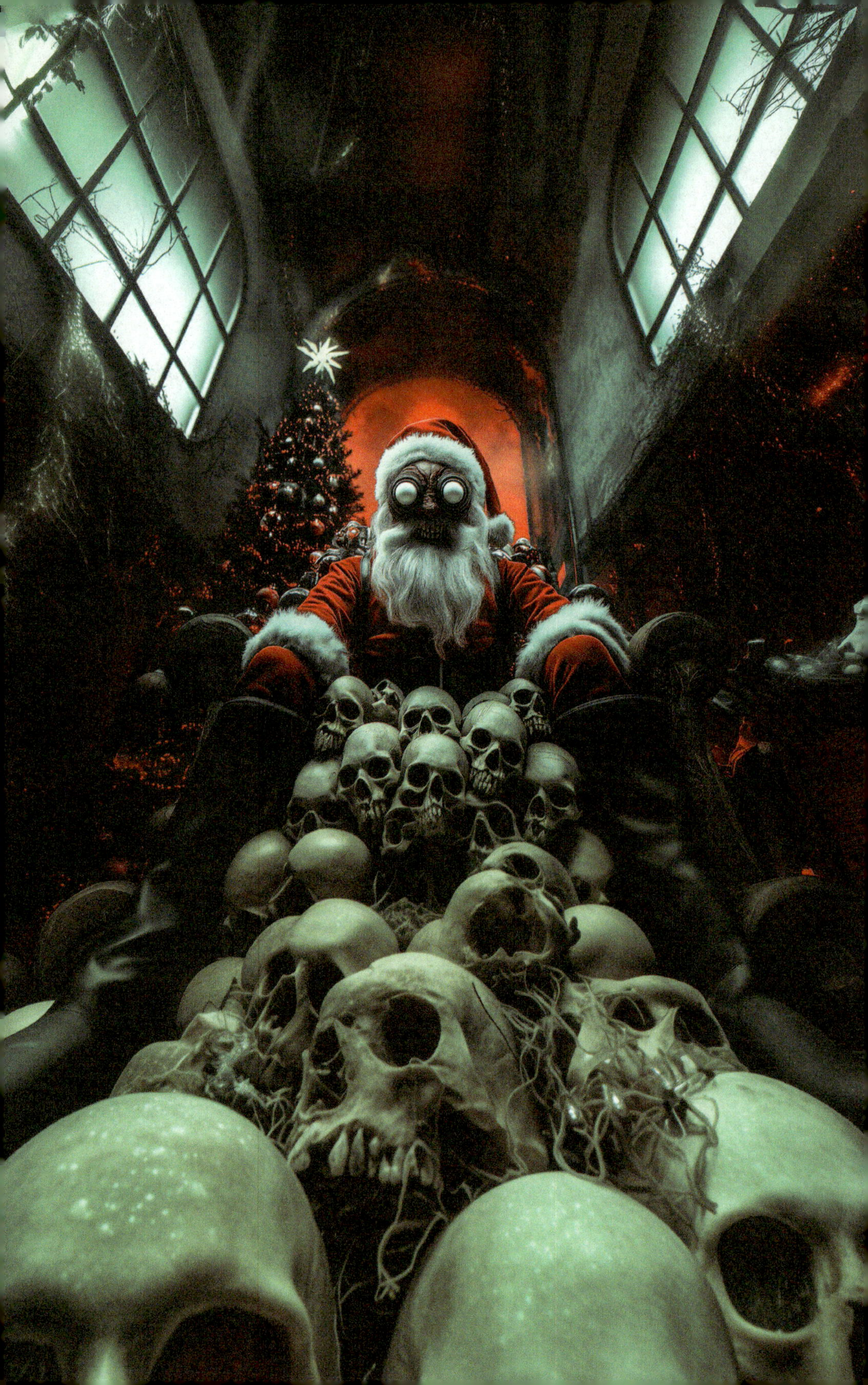

over them, but the rush felt wrong, twisting their insides. Ahead lay another maze, colder and darker, with strange symbols carved into the walls. They began to run, desperate to stay warm, slipping as Jake fell hard on the ice. Finally, they burst out into a clearing, shivering and gasping.

Before them loomed a massive castle, dark and imposing, with a glowing symbol carved into its front. They pushed inside, only to stumble upon a horrifying sight: a massive pile of elf skulls, stacked high with hollow eyes staring out. At the top sat a figure unlike any Santa they'd ever imagined. His eyes gleamed, his face a twisted mask of cruel delight, and his teeth looked far too sharp as he grinned down at them. Ethan felt his skin prickle and tighten, a plastic-like sheen creeping over his hands. He turned to Jake, whose face had frozen in terror—his cheeks, his eyes, hardening, taking on the glossy, doll-like surface of a toy. They looked at each other, horror dawning, as the figure at the top chuckled, leaning forward with a sinister smile.

"Did you like my dandy canes?" Santa's voice was deep and mocking, each word dripping with malice. "Welcome to my kingdom," he sneered. "There's plenty of work for you both at my factory. And you'll have all the candy canes you want…"

Santa's smile widened, his gaze dark and hungry. "…and in return, I get all I want from you. Every part of you… down to your very soul." Ethan looked again at the mountain of skulls beneath Santa's throne, and the terrible truth settled in his gut like ice: they would never leave this place.

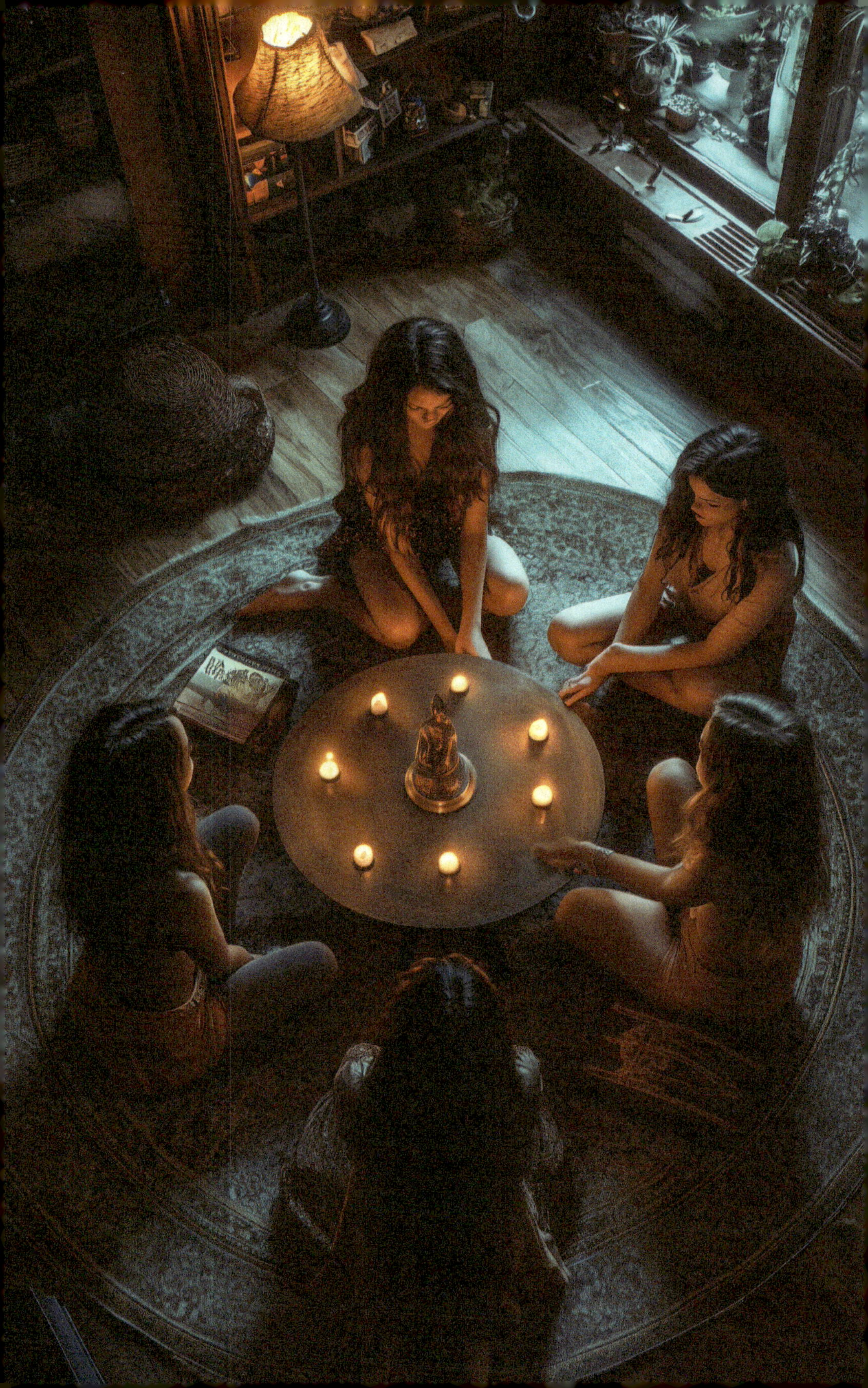

Karmic Debt

Sarah had heard the rumors about the "Karma" statuette. Whispers floated around school, claiming it could balance your deeds, good or bad. It was said that those who dared to perform a specific incantation in its presence would summon Karma itself, bringing judgment. If your wrongs outweighed your virtues, it would find you, demanding payment. It sounded like a sleepover ghost story, but when her friend Mindy invited her to try it, Sarah's curiosity got the better of her.

That night, she and four friends sat cross-legged on the floor of Mindy's dim living room. Seven candles flickered around the statuette on the table. The figure had no features—just a blank face that seemed to stare back. Trying to ignore her unease, Sarah joined in as they began the chant. It was an eerie rhyme, repeating like a twisted lullaby. By the fifth time, their voices blended together, the words slipping out almost automatically. Just as they finished the final verse, a

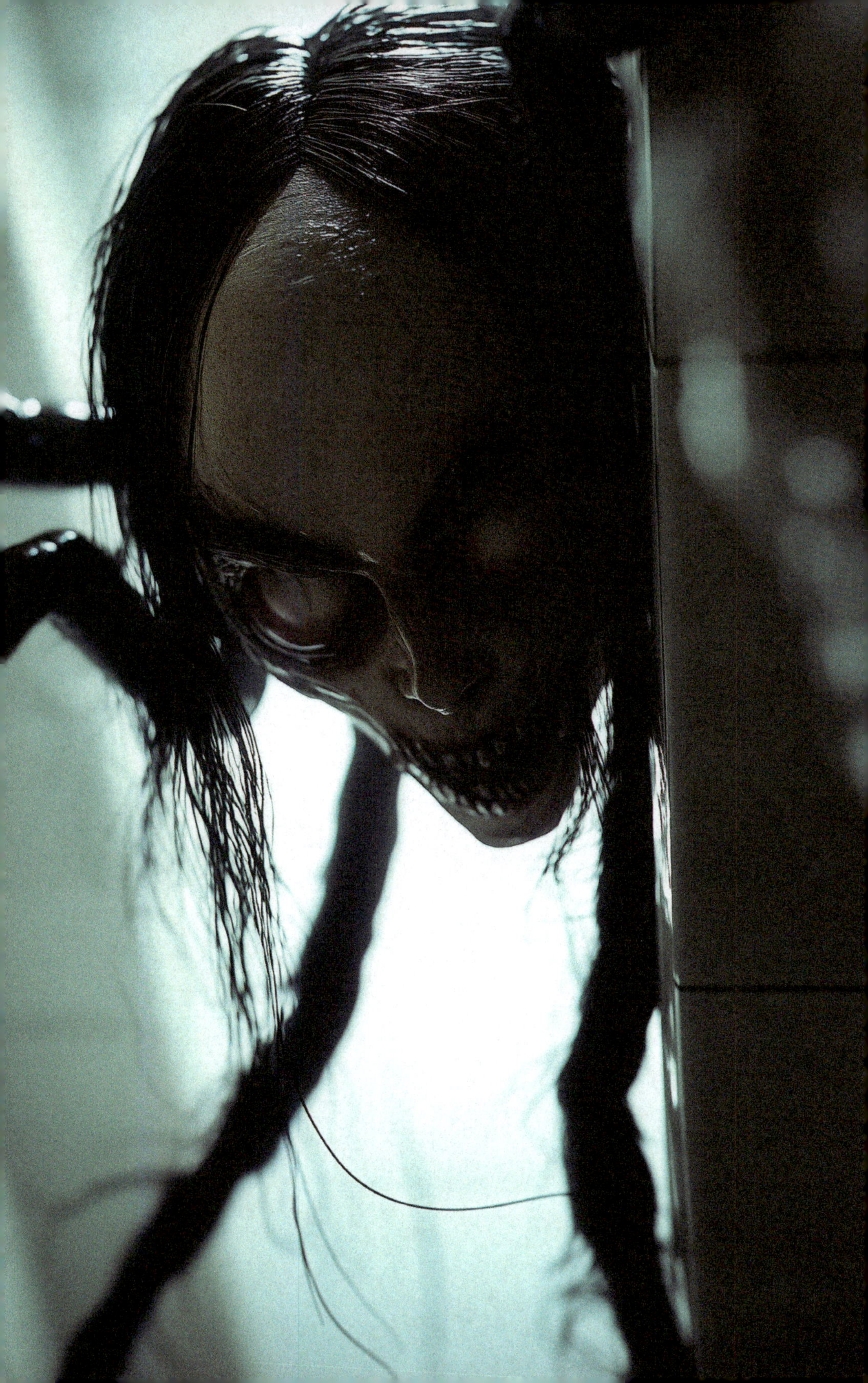

gust of wind blew in through the patio door, snuffing out the candles.

They all screamed, then burst into laughter. But while her friends calmed down, Sarah couldn't laugh. The dark room around her suddenly felt oppressive, as if something unseen were closing in. Her past mistakes filled her mind, like memories she couldn't escape. She thought of her ex-boyfriend, the rumors she'd spread to fit in, and the hurt she'd caused him.

She remembered the look in his eyes when he'd come to her after his mother passed, asking her to take him back. She had laughed and turned him away without a second thought. Now, surrounded by her friends, she felt a creeping sense of judgment, like someone—or something—was keeping score.

Overwhelmed, she stood up abruptly and made her way to the bathroom, hoping to clear her mind. She locked the door and splashed cold water on her face, breathing heavily. But as she looked up, her pulse raced. A faint shadow moved behind her in the mirror. She turned, scanning the small room, but saw nothing. Then, a soft whisper filled the air, sending chills down her spine.

"You owe me."

Her heart pounded as something crawled into view from behind the shower wall—a dark figure, spider-like, with a twisted, half-human face. Its eyes were blank and endless, fixed directly on her. She froze, unable to scream, as it crept

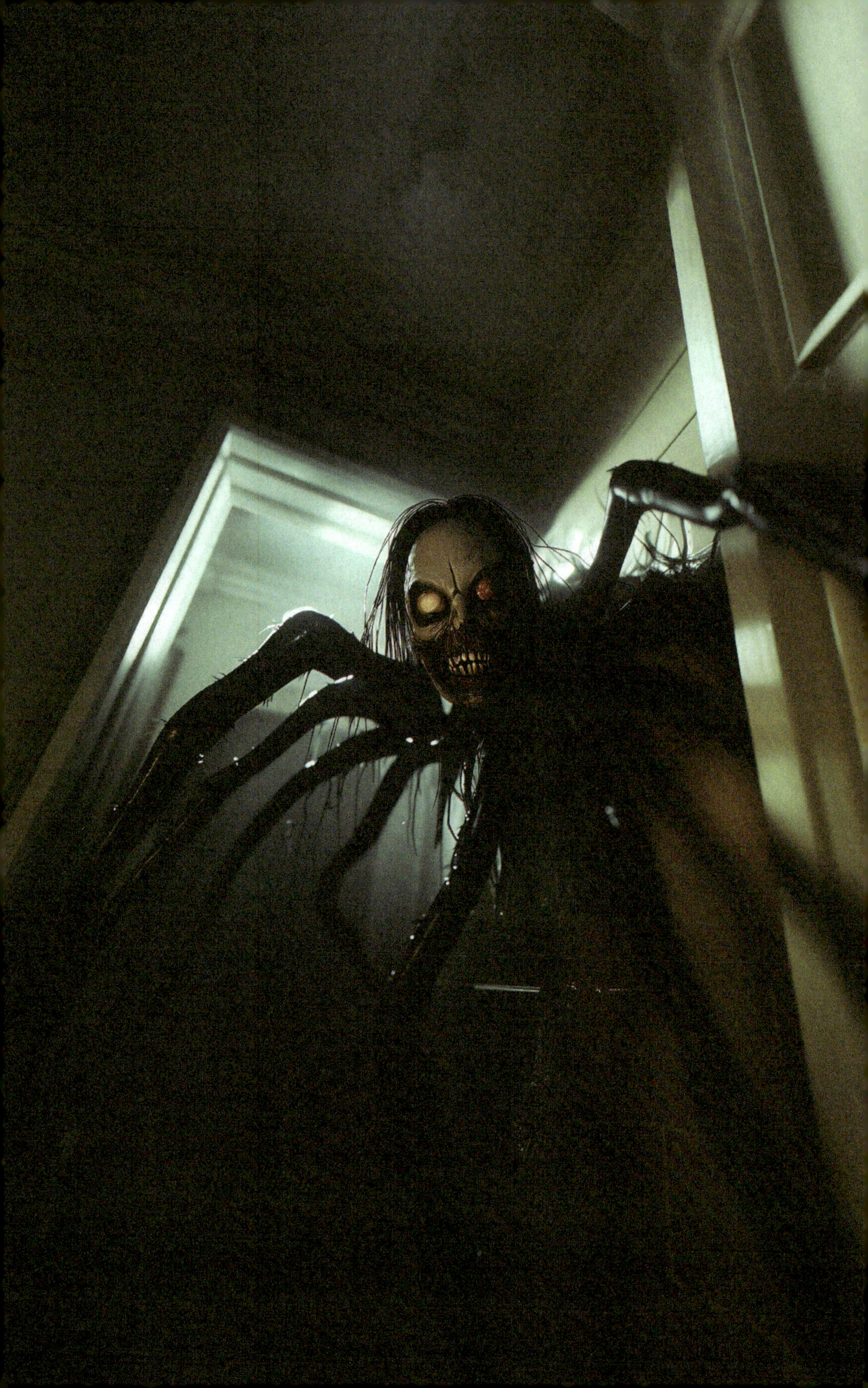

closer, its long legs tapping lightly on the tile. It whispered again, louder this time. "You owe me."

Panicking, Sarah lunged for the door, her hand trembling as she fumbled with the lock. But the creature moved faster, blocking her path. Its dark form loomed closer, filling her vision until all she could see was the empty, accusing stare. She shut her eyes, hoping it would vanish, but the whisper grew louder, echoing in her mind.

Outside, her friends exchanged uneasy glances. Sarah had been gone too long. Mindy walked over and knocked on the bathroom door, calling her name. There was no answer. Finally, she opened the door and looked inside.

The bathroom was empty.

Sarah was nowhere to be found, her phone lying on the counter, a faint mist clinging to the mirror. A silence settled over the group, each of them looking back at the statuette on the table. Its blank face seemed to gaze back, calm and watchful. Mindy could barely stand to look at it. She picked it up, hands shaking, and wrapped it in a cloth.

Without a word, she knew what she had to do. She would pass it on, hoping to leave the curse behind.

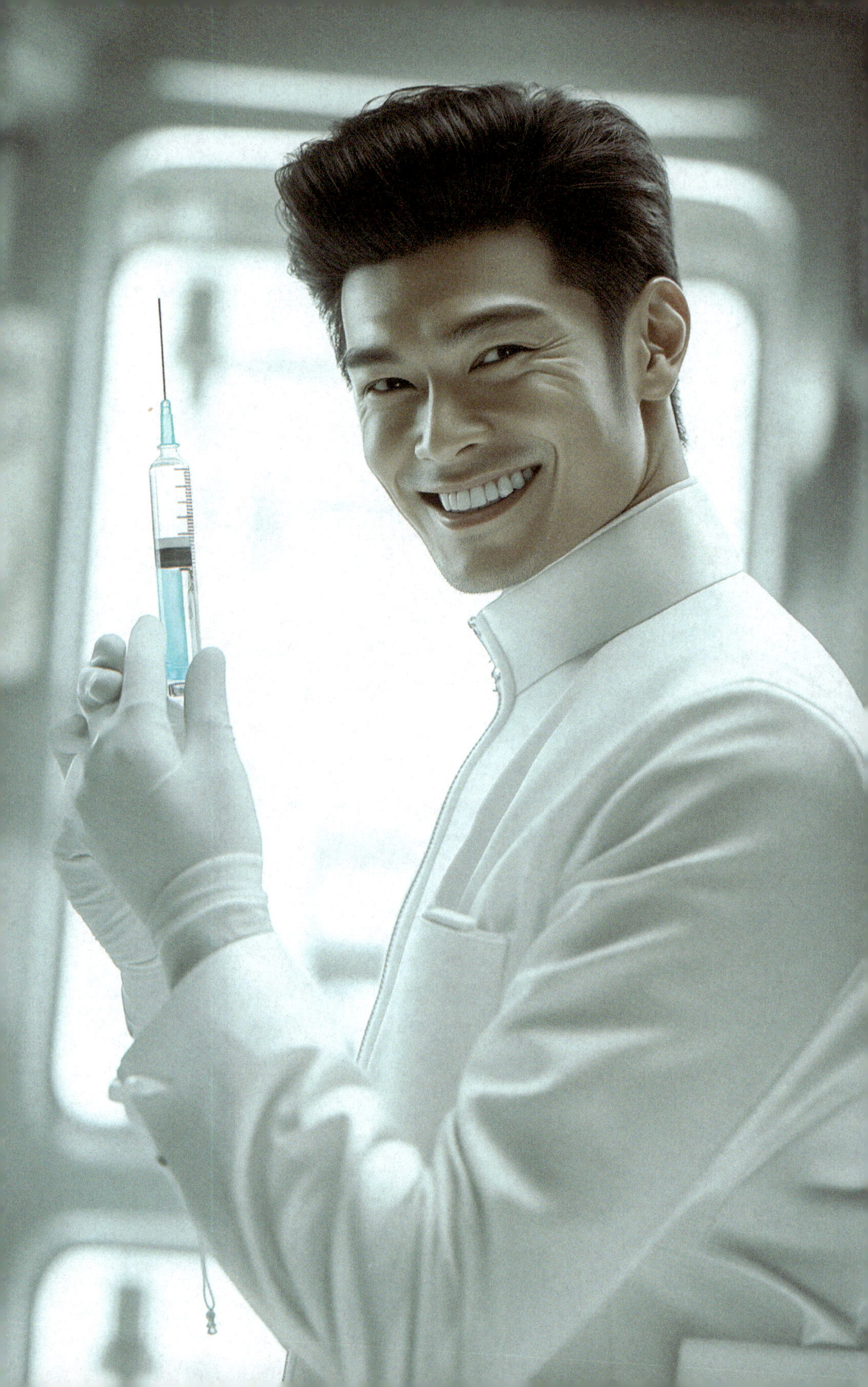

Pretty Please

In the dim light of a plastic surgery clinic, a beautiful woman sat waiting, her mind racing with anticipation. She had scraped together a bit of money, convinced that this visit could turn back the clock on her fading beauty. The clinic itself was an architectural marvel, its sterile white interior giving off an almost otherworldly vibe. As she stepped inside, a sense of excitement mingled with apprehension.

The receptionist greeted her with a smile and offered her a glass of water, which she declined. Instead, she settled into a plush chair in the waiting room, observing her surroundings. As an actress, the pressure to maintain her looks weighed heavily on her. She felt the encroaching shadows of age and longed to reclaim her youthful glow. The soothing music floated through the air, and the large television displayed images of transformed faces, igniting her imagination and fleeting hopes.

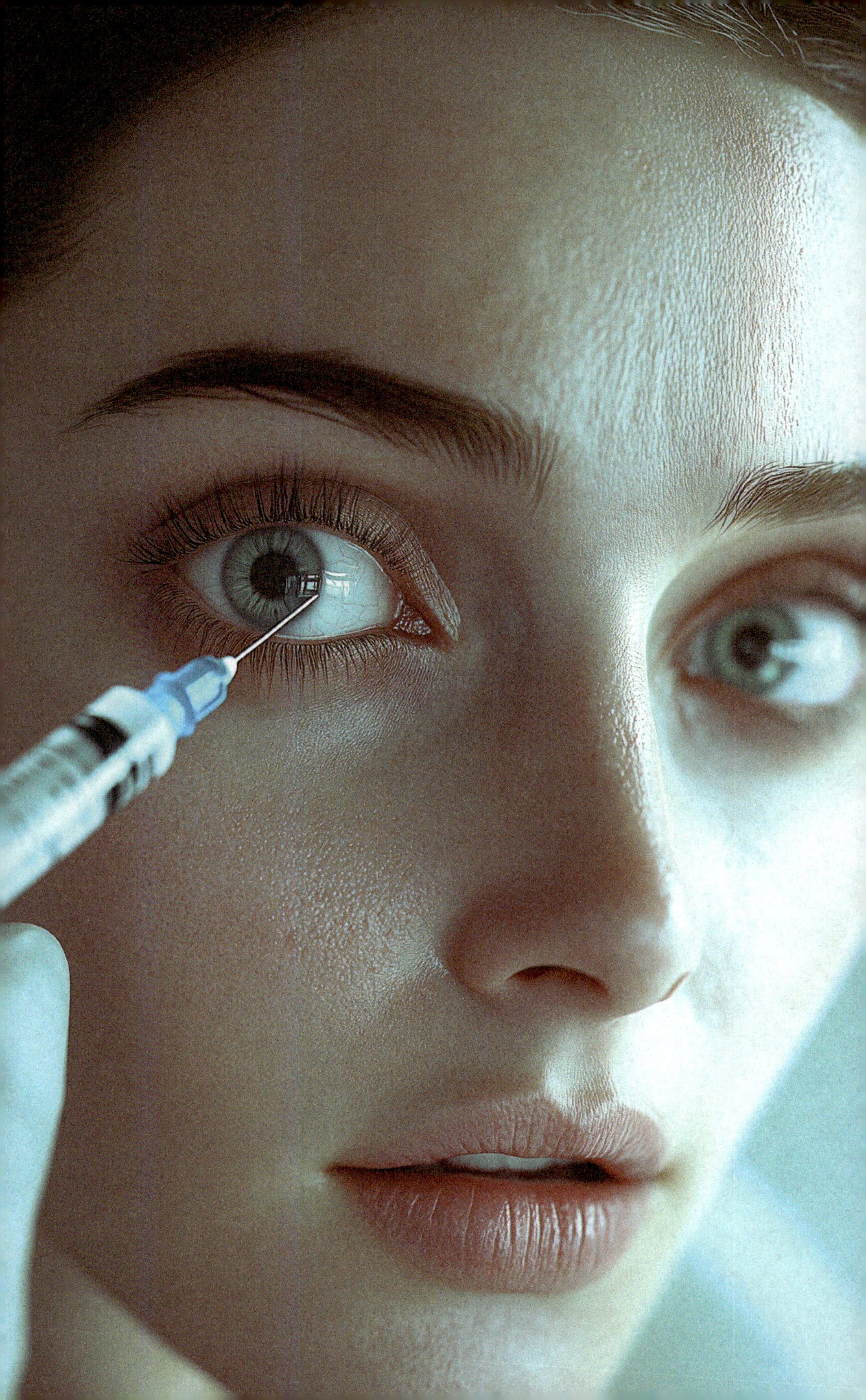

Her name was called, and she followed a nurse down a long hallway, engaging in small talk that barely registered. She couldn't shake the feeling that something was amiss, particularly with the digital posters showcasing before-and-after photos. There was an unsettling quality to the perfect smiles and smooth skin, but she brushed it aside, eager to hear what the surgeon would suggest.

Inside the consultation room, the nurse instructed her to sit in a chair, assuring her that Dr. Xiaolei would be with her shortly. The silence felt heavy as she pondered the potential pain and the scars that might follow. What would she tell her friends? Would they notice? Anxiety gripped her, and she could feel her hands trembling. Her mouth was dry from neglecting the offered water, but she chastised herself for letting nerves get the best of her.

Finally, Dr. Xiaolei entered with an air of confidence, charming her with his polished demeanor. He asked routine questions but moved quickly through them, explaining the procedures and pricing. She found herself nodding, excited by the prospect of discounted injections. As he began to work on her chin, his reassuring words filled the air, distracting her from the discomfort.

With each injection, she felt a combination of trepidation and hope. The doctor spoke enthusiastically about the advanced techniques he employed, urging her to let him know if she felt any discomfort. When she mentioned a blurring in her vision, he brushed it off as normal, and she found her-

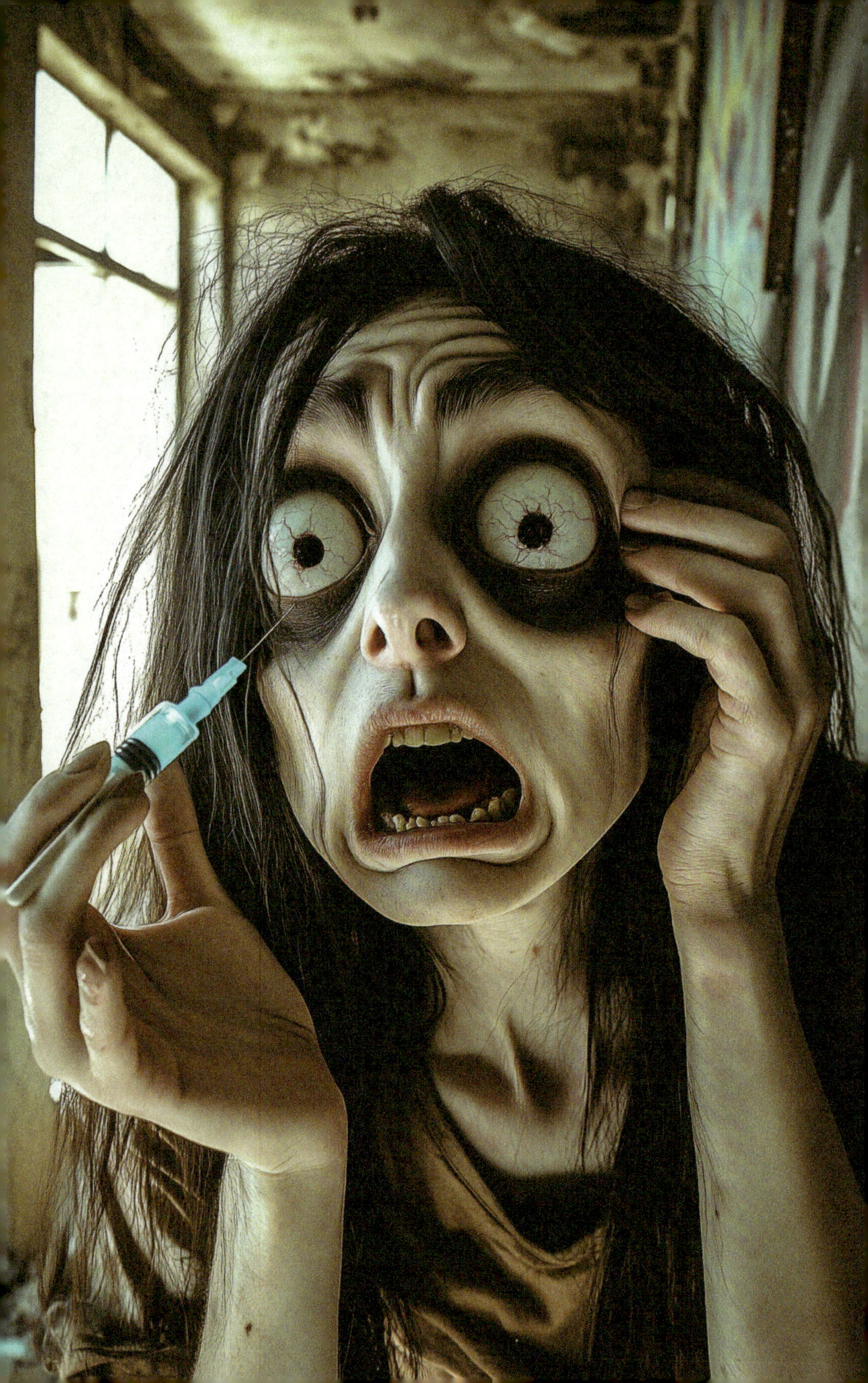

self growing dizzier, closing her eyes to escape the reality of what was happening.

Suddenly, she was jolted awake, her heart racing. Looking in the mirror, panic washed over her as she recognized the reflection staring back. Her eyes were unnaturally large, her features grotesque and distorted. What had she done? Stepping closer, her heart sank as she caught sight of a syringe clutched tightly in her hand. Her skin bore a multitude of tiny puncture marks, each one a reminder of her hasty decision. "What have I done?" she gasped, her mind spiraling.

A flash of clarity broke through her panic, revealing the truth: she wasn't a glamorous actress at all, but rather a homeless woman lost in a haze of drugs. The clinic, the beauty she longed for, was nothing more than a hallucination fueled by desperation and addiction. The memories flooded back—the crumbling ruins where she squatted, the discarded syringes she had used to escape reality. In that moment, the illusion shattered, and the weight of her existence pressed down hard. She was not the woman she imagined; she was a ghost, drifting through life, haunted by the choices she had made.

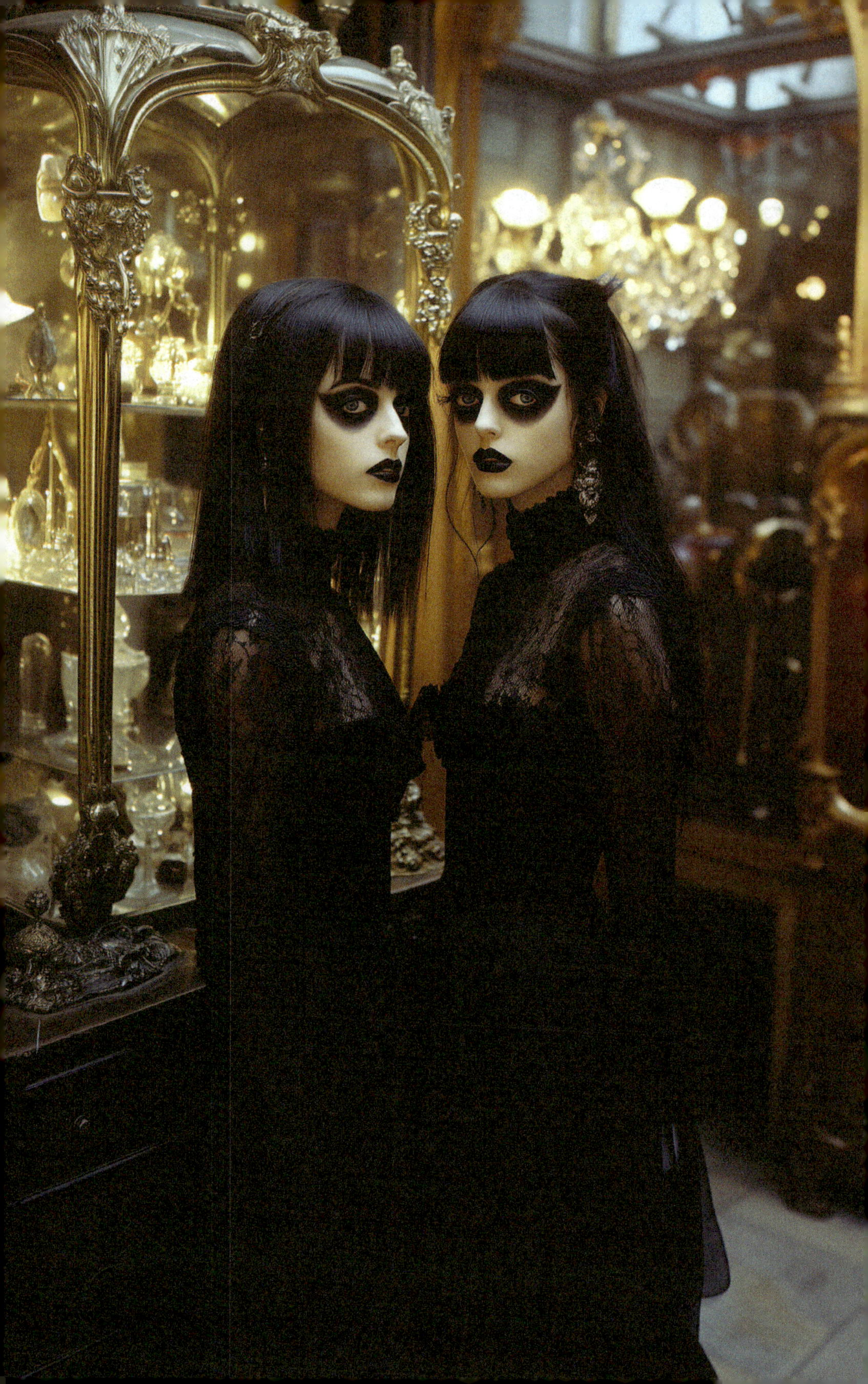

Finger Eater

Tatiana and her friend Marla walked toward the ominous front doors of Sterling's, a peculiar little shop infamous for its strange and sometimes unsettling trinkets. Marla had suggested they come here to buy a finger trap, one of those simple puzzle devices that binds two fingers until the user figures out the trick to get free. Their plan was to prank an obnoxious friend.

The rumors surrounding Sterling's floated into Tatiana's mind as she walked. Some people said that the store's items were cursed, imbued with the kind of mischief that punished those who used them with bad intentions. But Marla seemed unfazed, calm even, as she strode ahead.

Inside, they found the finger trap—a flimsy-looking cylinder priced much higher than Tatiana remembered. They didn't have enough money between them to buy it. Marla, her eyes narrowing with determination, whispered that she'd just steal it. Tatiana's gaze darted around, scanning the store

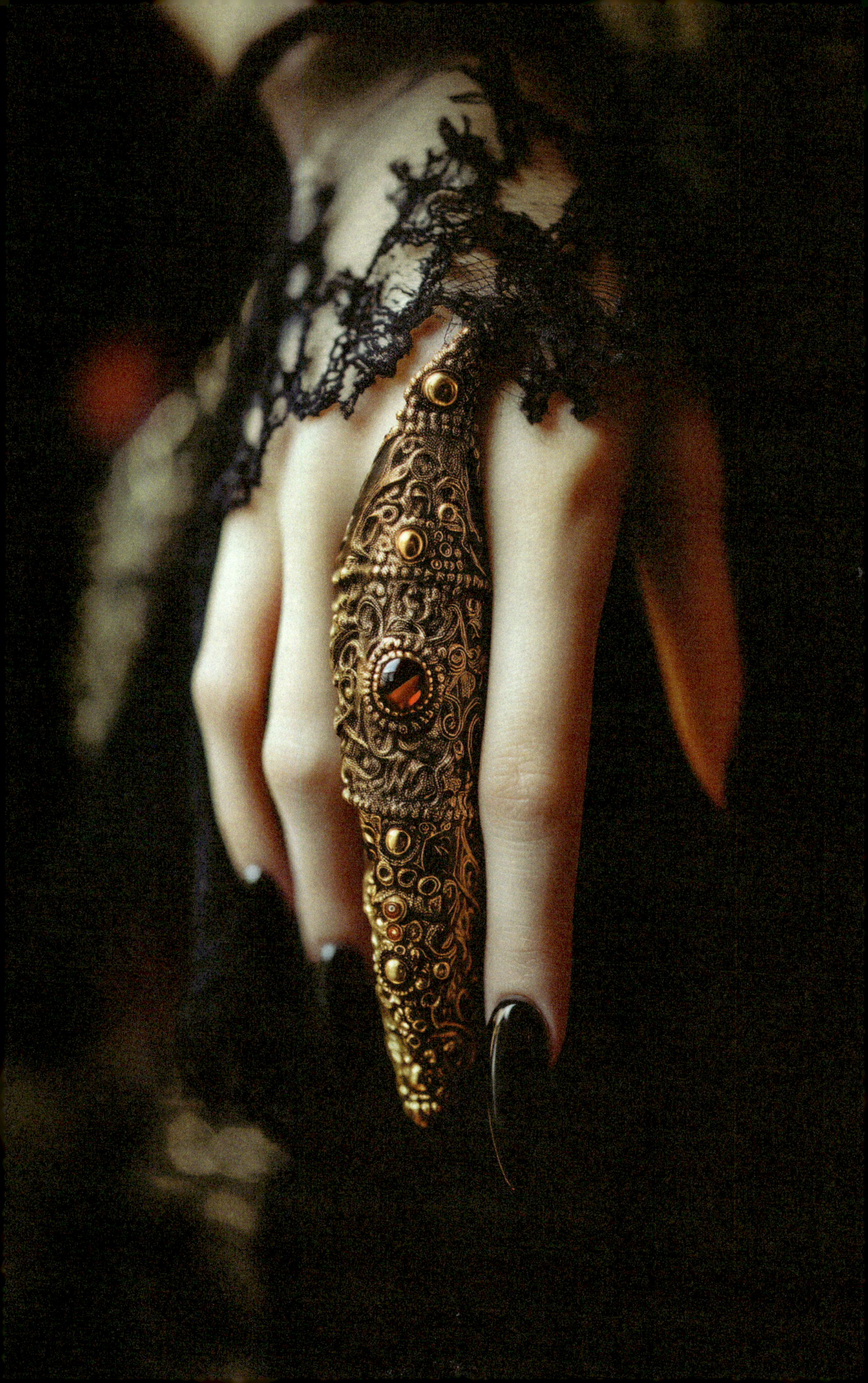

for witnesses. Marla swiftly slipped the finger trap into her purse, and they both turned to leave, trying to keep their movements casual.

A deep voice stopped them in their tracks. They turned slowly to see the owner—a tall, lanky man whose face was hidden behind reflective glasses. Marla smiled nervously, muttering something about just browsing, while Tatiana stood frozen, nodding mechanically. The man seemed oblivious to their little theft, or at least he gave no sign that he'd noticed. He murmured a polite farewell and moved on to help another customer.

They left the store, breathing easier, and stopped just a few feet away, out of the owner's line of sight. Marla, looking a little shaken, rummaged in her purse. She frowned, muttering that she couldn't find the finger trap and couldn't even remember where she'd put it. But then, her face went pale.

"Something... just grabbed my finger," she whispered.

Tatiana's stomach twisted as Marla slowly pulled her hand from the bag. There, wrapped tightly around her finger, was the finger trap. But something was wrong. The material seemed to be pulsing, almost breathing, like it had a life of its own. Marla yanked at it, her breath quickening as she struggled to free herself. But instead of loosening, the trap began to lengthen, sliding over her hand, then crawling steadily up her wrist, wrapping her skin as if alive.

"Get it off me!" Marla cried, her voice high and shaking.

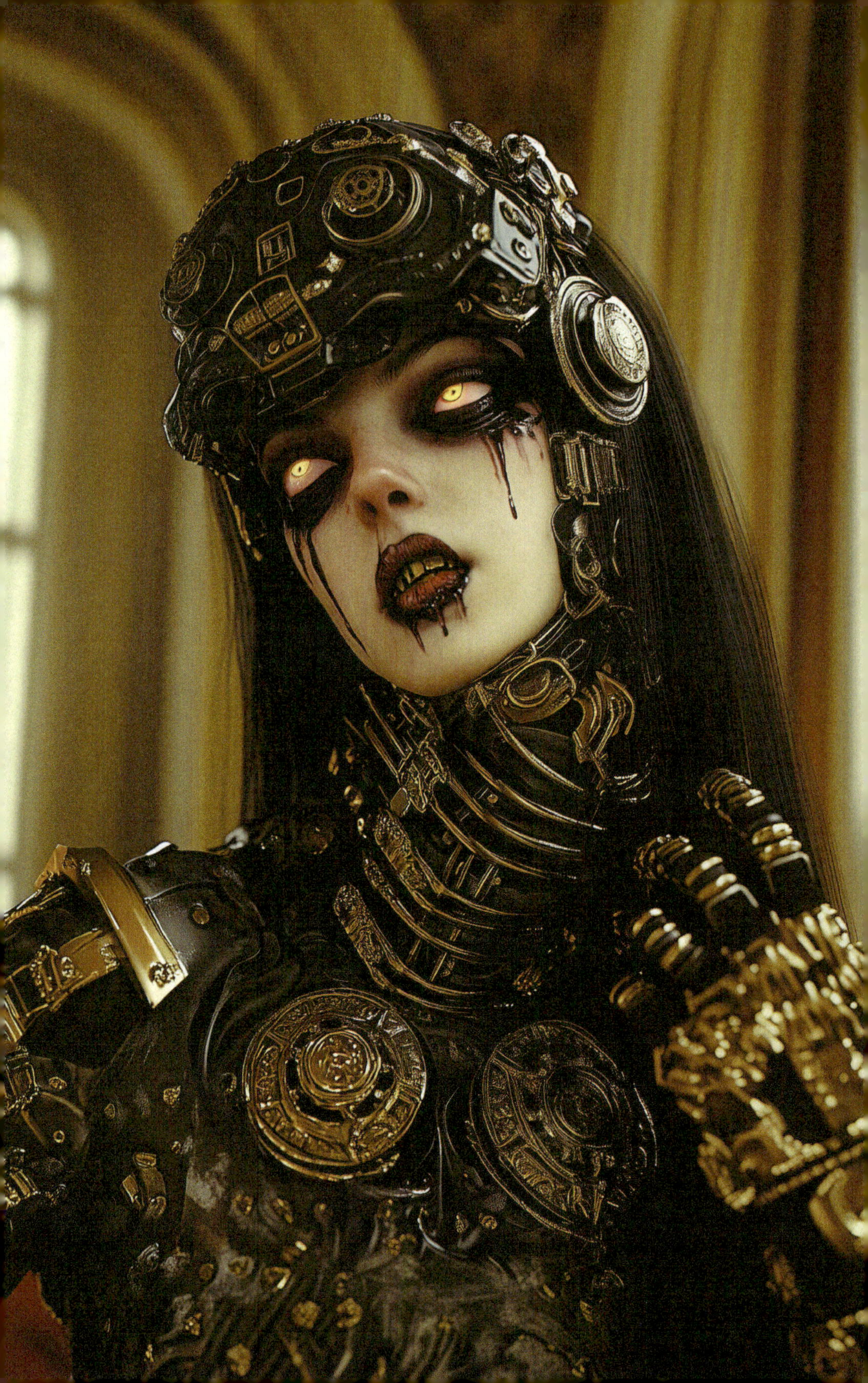

Tatiana grabbed her by the wrist, desperately tugging at the trap, but it only wound tighter, now coiling around Marla's forearm. Frantically, Marla shoved a small pair of scissors into Tatiana's hand, her fingers trembling too much to use them herself. Tatiana leaned in, her own hands shaking as she tried to slice the fabric away. But with each cut, the trap seemed to repair itself, stretching and twisting further up Marla's arm.

Now the thing was creeping over her shoulder, spiraling across her torso like a thick, unbreakable vine. Tatiana's heartbeat thundered as she tried to pull the fabric away from Marla's neck, but it was like trying to tear steel. She couldn't breathe; she could hardly see straight as the trap wound itself up, twisting around Marla's throat, her terrified face barely visible through the constricting layers.

Tatiana tugged and pulled, but the trap had a will of its own, consuming Marla inch by inch, wrapping around her completely. In the silent, empty hallway outside Sterling's, Marla's terrified eyes disappeared under the final layer of fabric, leaving Tatiana alone, breathless and trembling, with nothing left to hold on to.

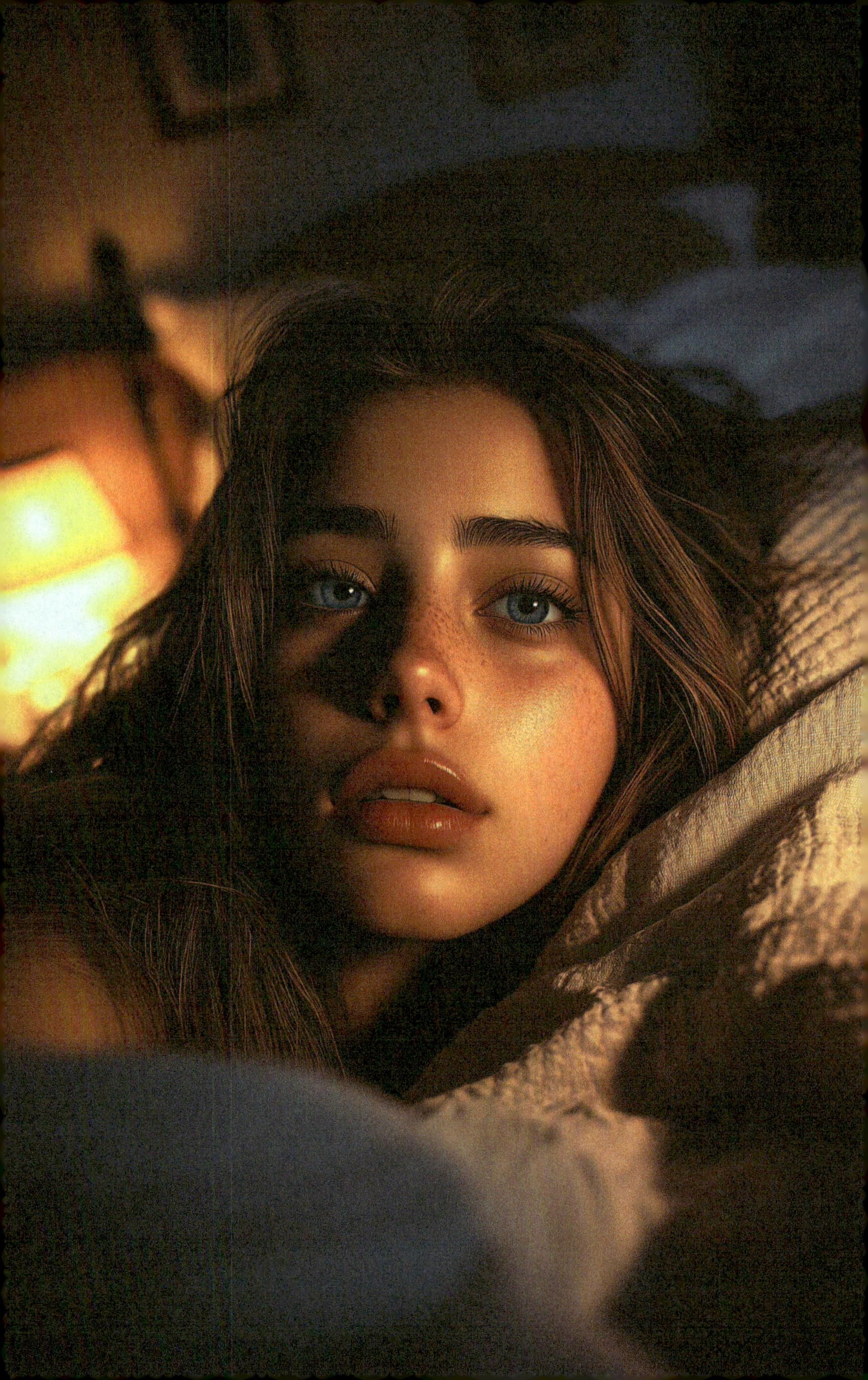

Closet Dweller

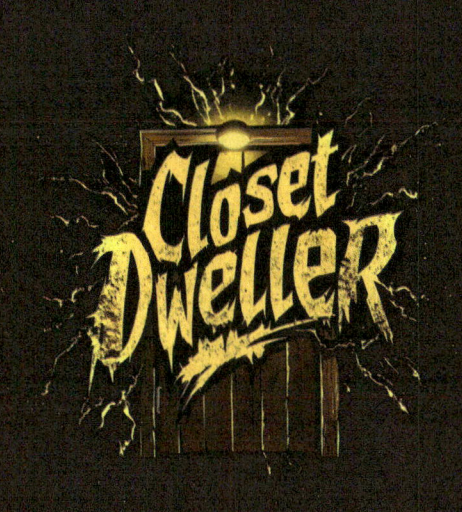

She stared at the closet door, her ears straining to catch the faint scratching sounds that crept through the silence. For weeks, the noises had returned each night, growing louder, more persistent, until they became an unrelenting presence that disturbed her every thought and robbed her of sleep. Each scrape sent a chill down her spine, a reminder that something was lurking just beyond her reach, taunting her with its presence.

She tried to convince herself it was a mouse or some small rodent, though a deep unease settled in her stomach. The thought made her skin crawl. She was exhausted, her nights slipping by in a haze of fractured sleep and anxious silence, the shadows in her room growing longer and more menacing. But tonight, she decided she'd had enough. She was going to find out what was making those sounds.

With a deep breath, she stepped toward the closet. As her hand neared the door, the scratching stopped, leaving only

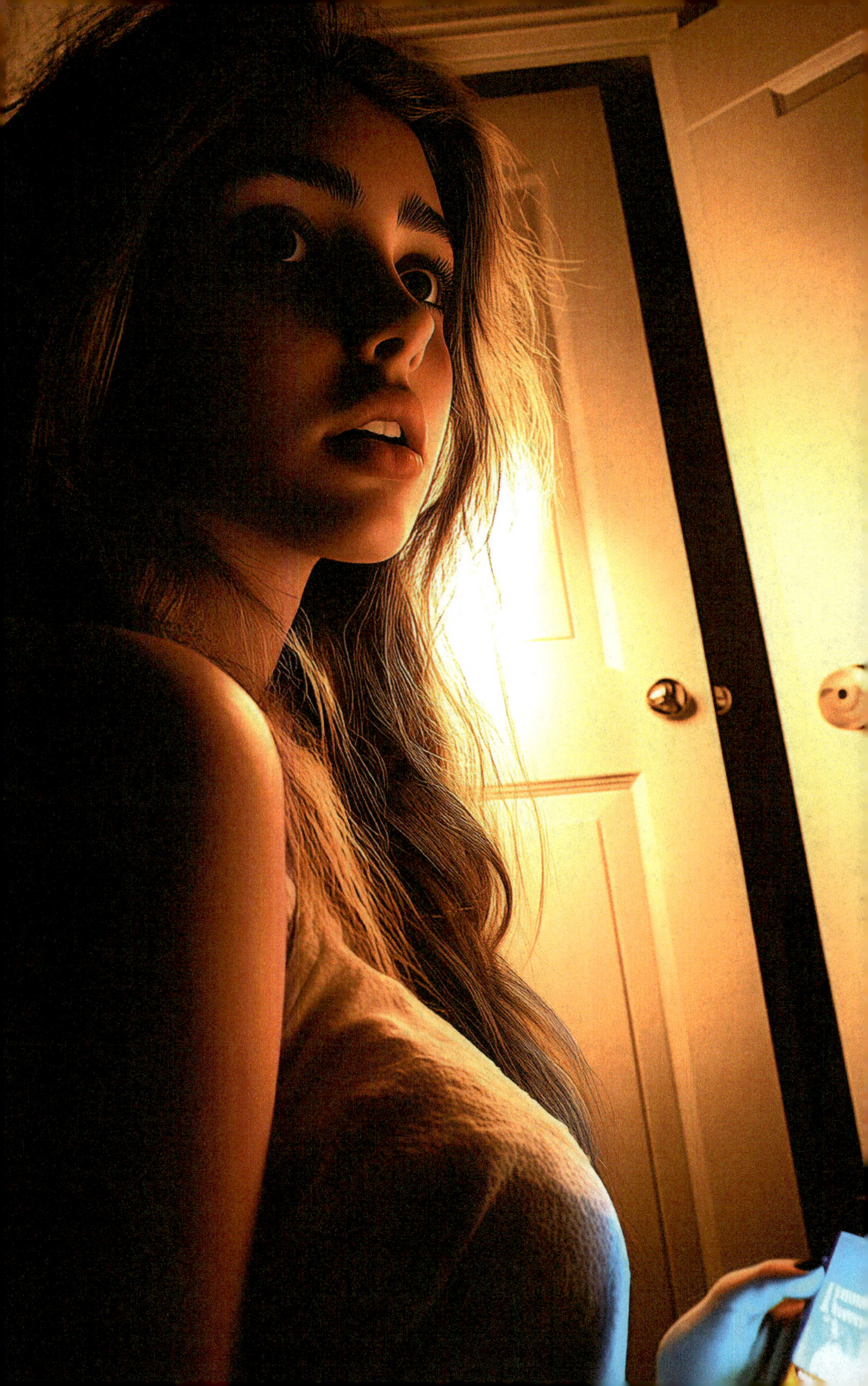

the soft hum of the night, as if the air itself had gone still, holding its breath in anticipation. She swallowed hard, her fingers hovering over the handle, then opened the door and flicked on the light. The pale glow filled the closet, revealing only clothes, shoes, and the usual clutter. But the silence felt heavy, pressing against her ears as she scanned the shelves and corners, searching for something that wasn't there. After a moment, she turned off the light, leaving the door open just a crack, hoping that would be enough to let her sleep.

But as she crawled back into bed, the scratching started again, echoing through the darkness like a sinister lullaby. She clenched her fists, staring at the door with irritation mixed with dread, each scratch seeming to claw at her sanity. She was too tired to keep listening to this sound that she was certain only grew louder by the second, a relentless reminder of her growing fear. Her heartbeat quickened, and her breath caught in her throat as she noticed a shadow shift inside the closet, a darkness that seemed to pulse with malevolence.

Gathering her courage, she slipped out of bed and walked toward the door, her legs trembling, each step feeling heavier as if the air around her was thickening. She pushed the door slowly, steeling herself for whatever lay beyond, heart pounding like a drum in her ears.

Inside the closet, a creature lurked, its form both skeletal and plant-like, with twisted branches resembling brittle bones, reaching out as if yearning for her. Empty eye sock-

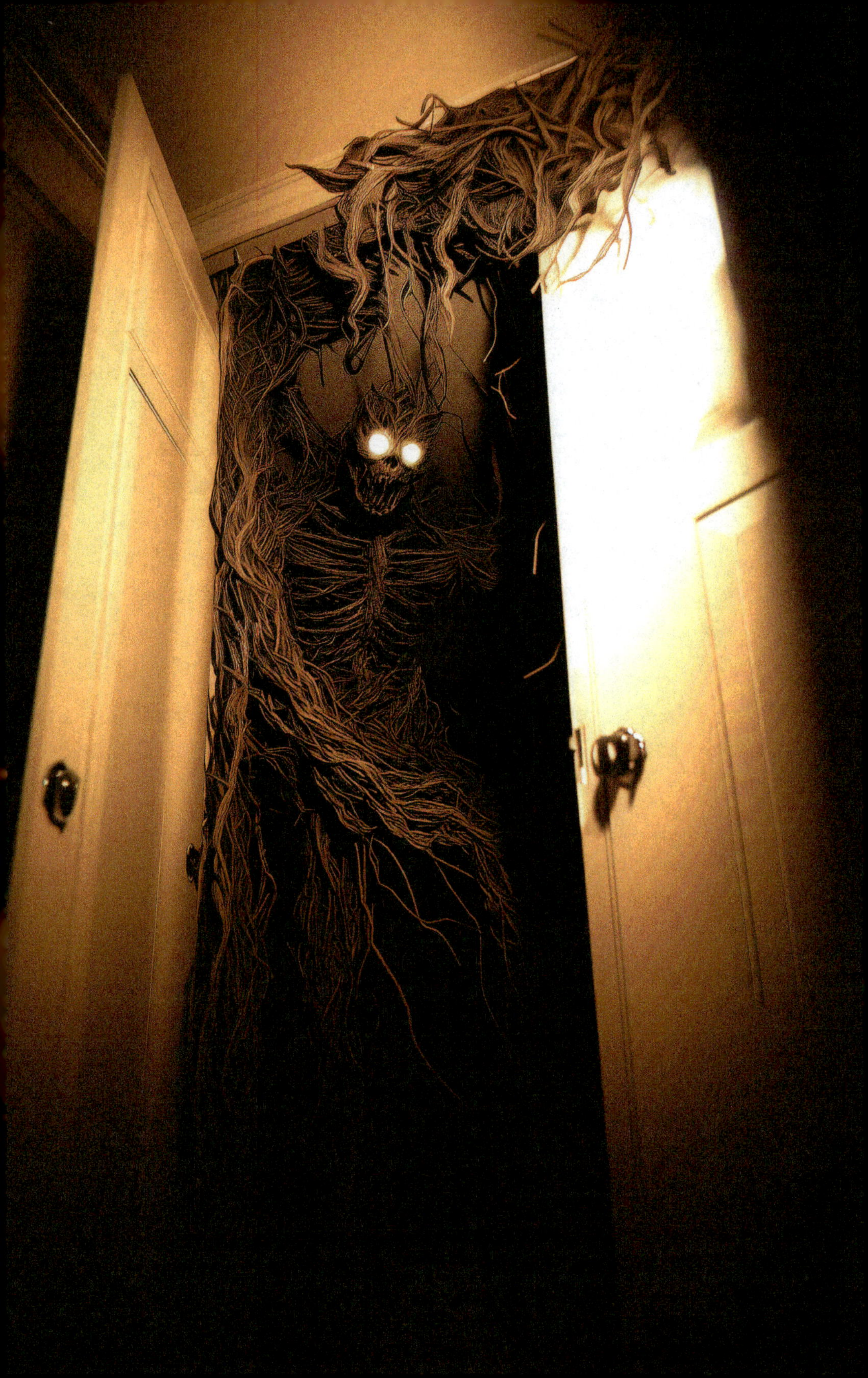

ets glowed faintly, casting an eerie light that made her skin crawl. As she stood frozen, horrified, it shifted, and she saw roots crawling along the walls and ceiling, anchoring it to the very fabric of her room.

The rustling grew louder, and her breath caught as she noticed something strange. Reflected faintly in the creature's hollow eye sockets was her own face, twisted and unfamiliar, staring back at her. She took a step back, heart pounding, but then it spoke—in her own voice, sweet yet dripping with malice.

"Are you ready?" it whispered, grinning wider, a sound that felt like a knife cutting through the air. "Ready to come inside?"

The scratching hadn't been random at all. It had been an invitation.

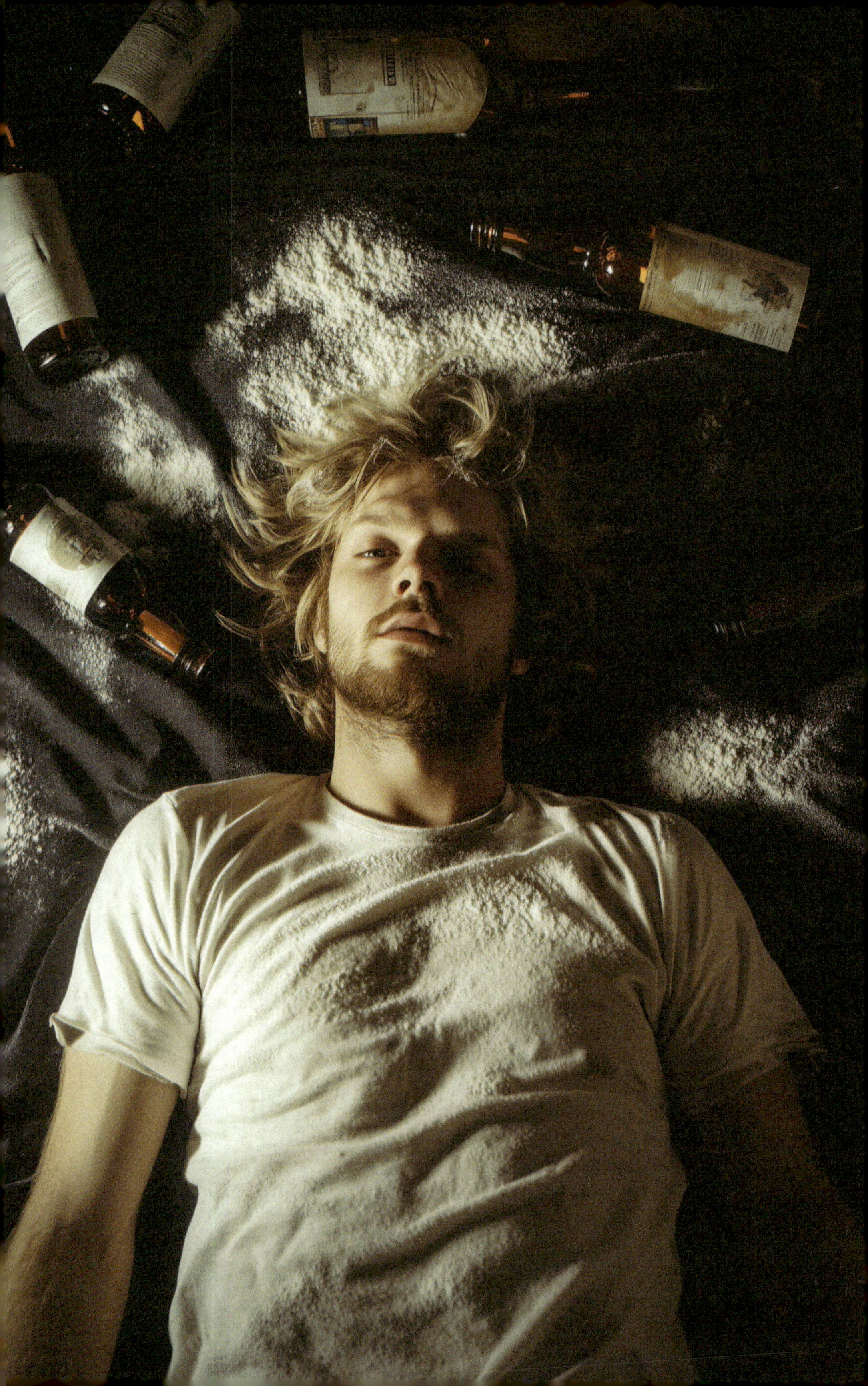

Imaginary Fiends

Braden woke up to the dull throb of a hangover, the kind that felt like a lead weight in his skull. The room was a mess—empty bottles cluttered the floor, and white powder lay scattered across the bed and nightstand, remnants of a night he could barely recall. Groaning, he rolled over, trying to shake off the fog of confusion.

As he tried to sit up, laughter floated through the air. Two female voices were giggling in the bathroom. He squinted at the clock, struggling to remember who had been there with him last night. It was all a blur. Ignoring the pain in his back, he pushed himself off the bed and stumbled toward the bathroom, curiosity and dread mingling in his gut.

When he stepped inside, he found his two childhood imaginary friends standing there, grinning at him. They had been gone for a year, and he thought they were lost to him forever. Now they looked different—older and twisted, like something out of a nightmare. Yet, as he looked at them, he felt a famil-

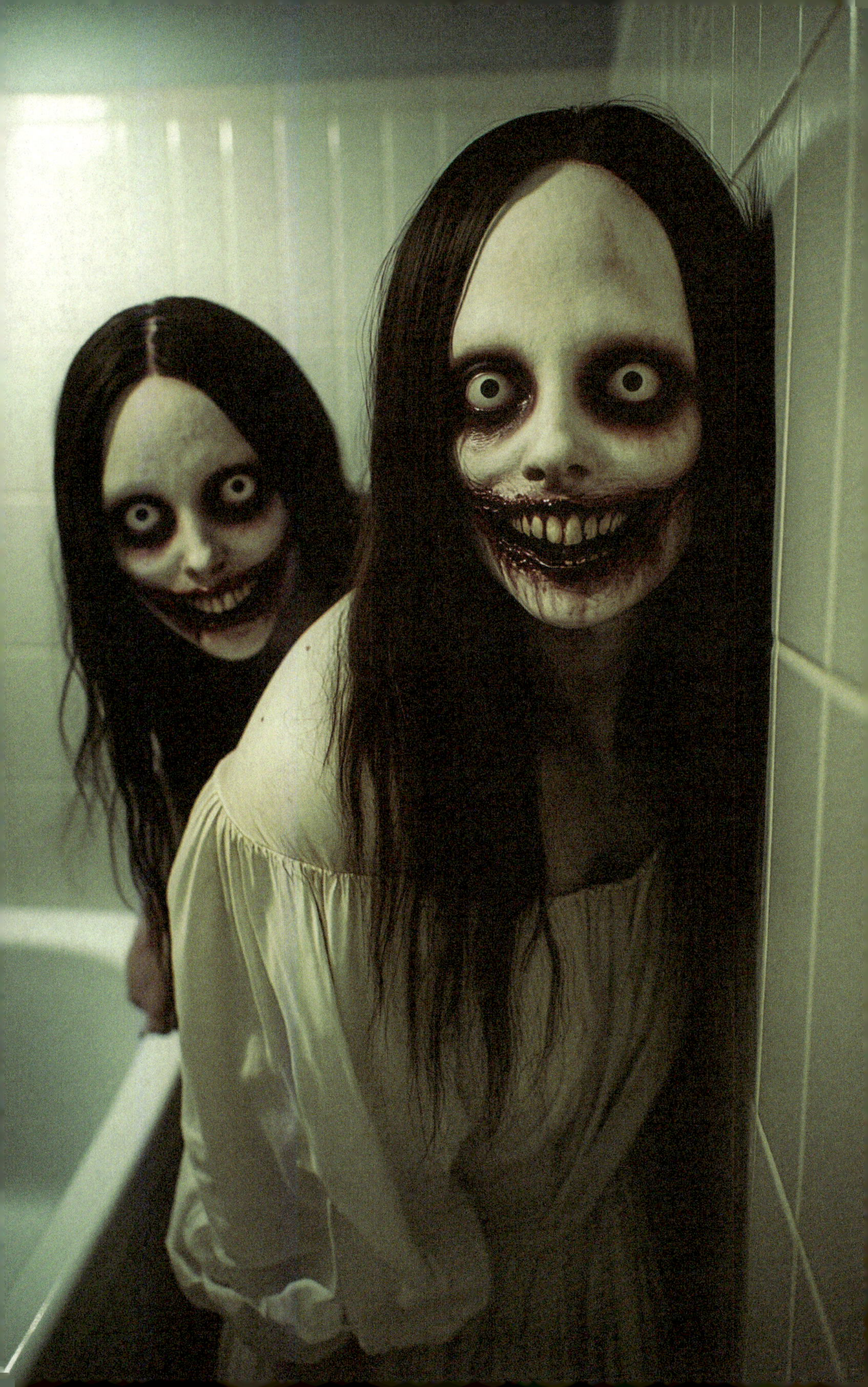

iar, unsettling attraction, a pull he couldn't explain. They had aged alongside him over the years, and now, despite their warped appearances, he couldn't deny that part of him still found them alluring.

"We missed you," one of them said, her voice dripping with sweetness that felt wrong. She stepped closer, her eyes gleaming with mischief, as if they held secrets only they could share. "Did you miss us, Braden? You know, we were always the best part of your life. Look at us. We've grown up just like you." She twirled a finger through her tangled hair, leaning in slightly, as if testing the waters of his desire, her breath warm against his skin. "Do you still find us pretty?"

The question hung in the air, heavy with unspoken promises and unrelenting darkness. She smiled wider, revealing teeth that were sharper than he remembered, their edges glinting like shards of glass. The other one took a step closer, her expression a mix of playful seduction and something sinister, her voice low and inviting. "You could have everything you've ever wanted with us, Braden. Just let us show you..." The lure of their words wrapped around him like a warm blanket, but he felt a knot of fear tightening in his stomach, a warning that this reunion was anything but harmless.

The words sent a chill down his spine. He shuffled to the kitchen, anxiety coiling tighter in his stomach. What surprise could they have in store for him?

When he entered, he froze. A living room chair stood in the center of the room, a rope hanging from the ceiling above

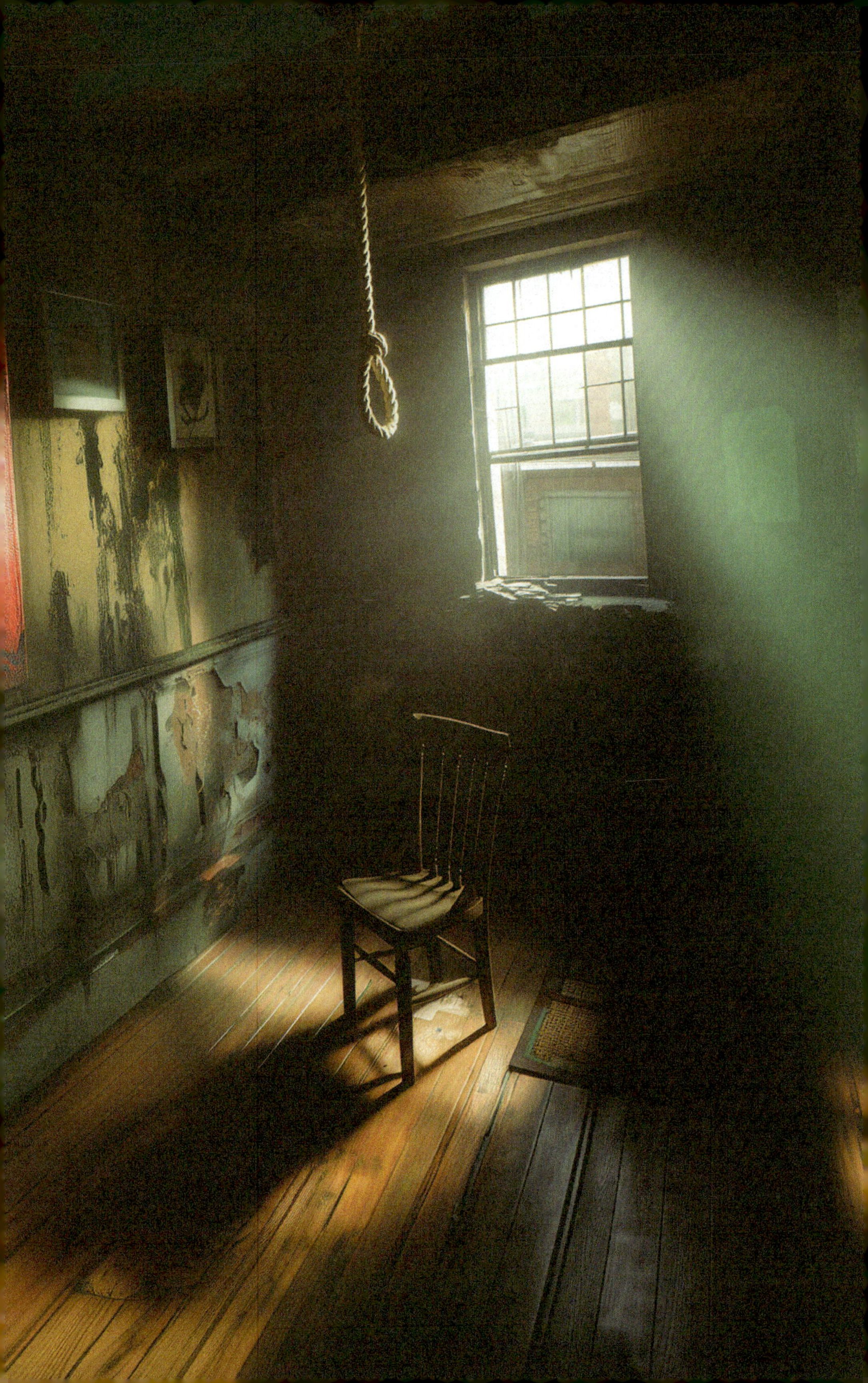

it. At the end of the rope was a noose, swinging slightly as if someone had just left it there. His heart raced as he processed the scene.

The laughter from the bathroom erupted again, filling the space with a haunting echo. "Join us, Braden!" they called out, their voices sweet yet chilling. "It's so much better on the other side. You've always wanted to escape, haven't you?"

He looked at the rope, its purpose clear and terrifying. They were always so convincing, those girls. A wave of panic washed over him as he stumbled backward, the seductive pull of their words mingling with an overwhelming sense of dread, urging him to embrace the darkness they offered.

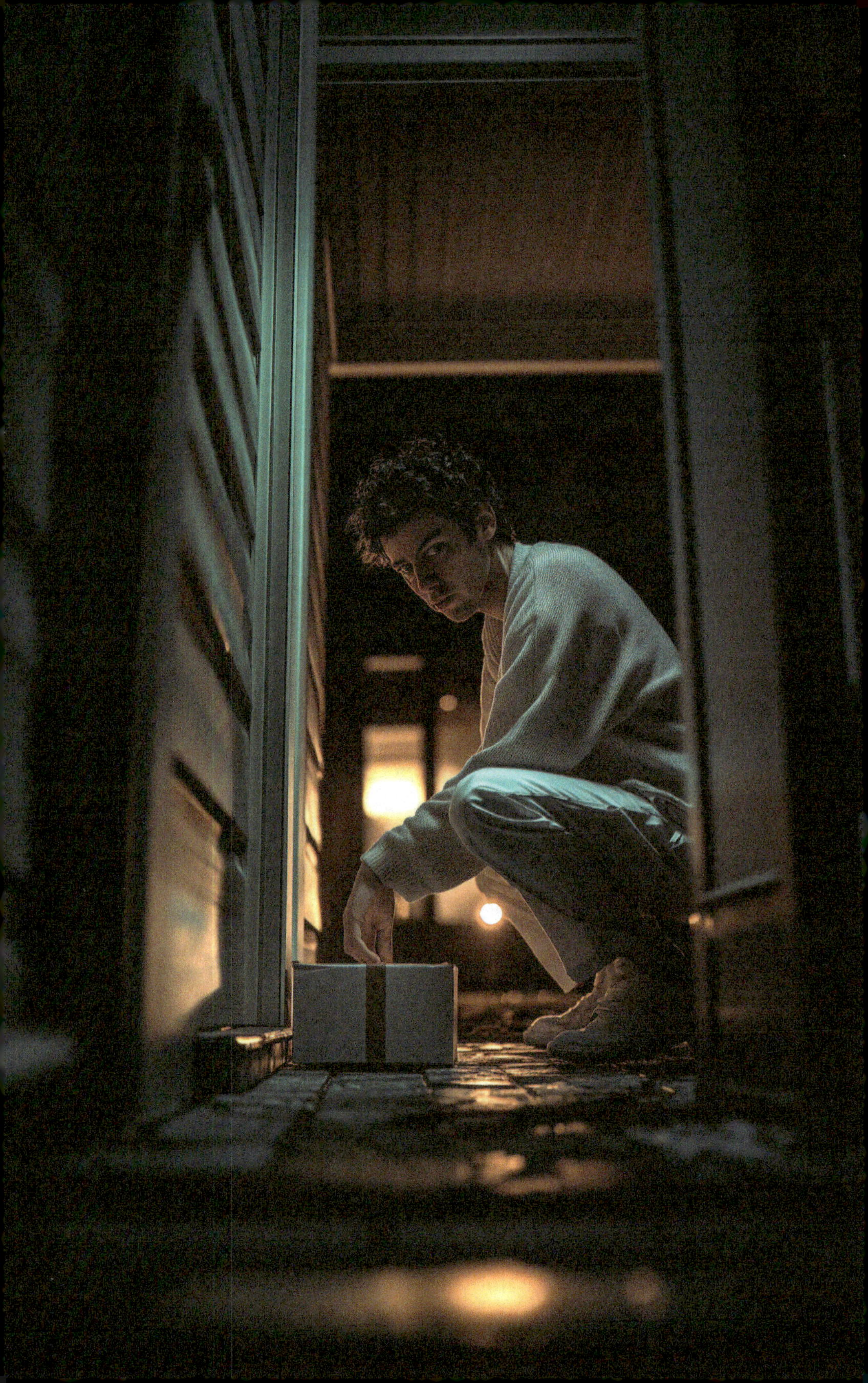

Endless Confinement

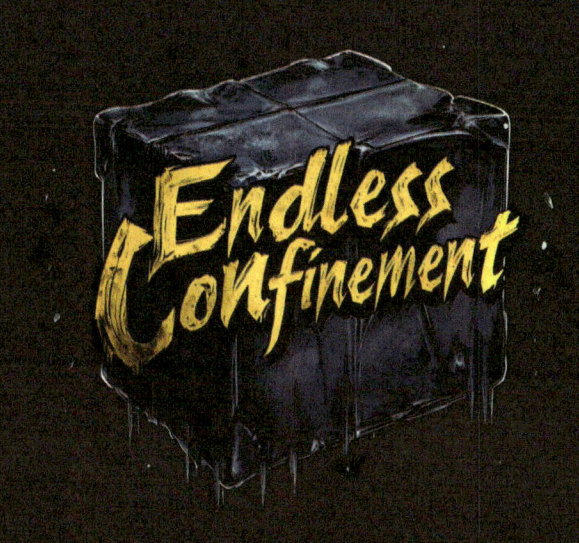

He had no idea how long he'd been trapped here—two days, maybe more. His memories of how he'd arrived were nothing but a haze. Every attempt to piece it together circled back to a single act: stealing a package from the old man's porch, convinced it would be easy. The man was strange, a survivalist type with unsettling signs plastered all over his house. Yet the details of that day faded quickly, overshadowed by a gnawing hunger and the oppressive fear of this cramped metal box where he'd awakened.

There wasn't even room to stand. A single white neon light buzzed above him, casting a harsh glow over the cold, unyielding metal walls. Under that stark illumination, a thought began to take shape. If he could shatter the light, perhaps the glass would provide a way out. He imagined gripping a sharp piece, felt its edge in his mind, a thin line separating freedom from something darker. It was a last resort, a grim escape glowing just out of reach.

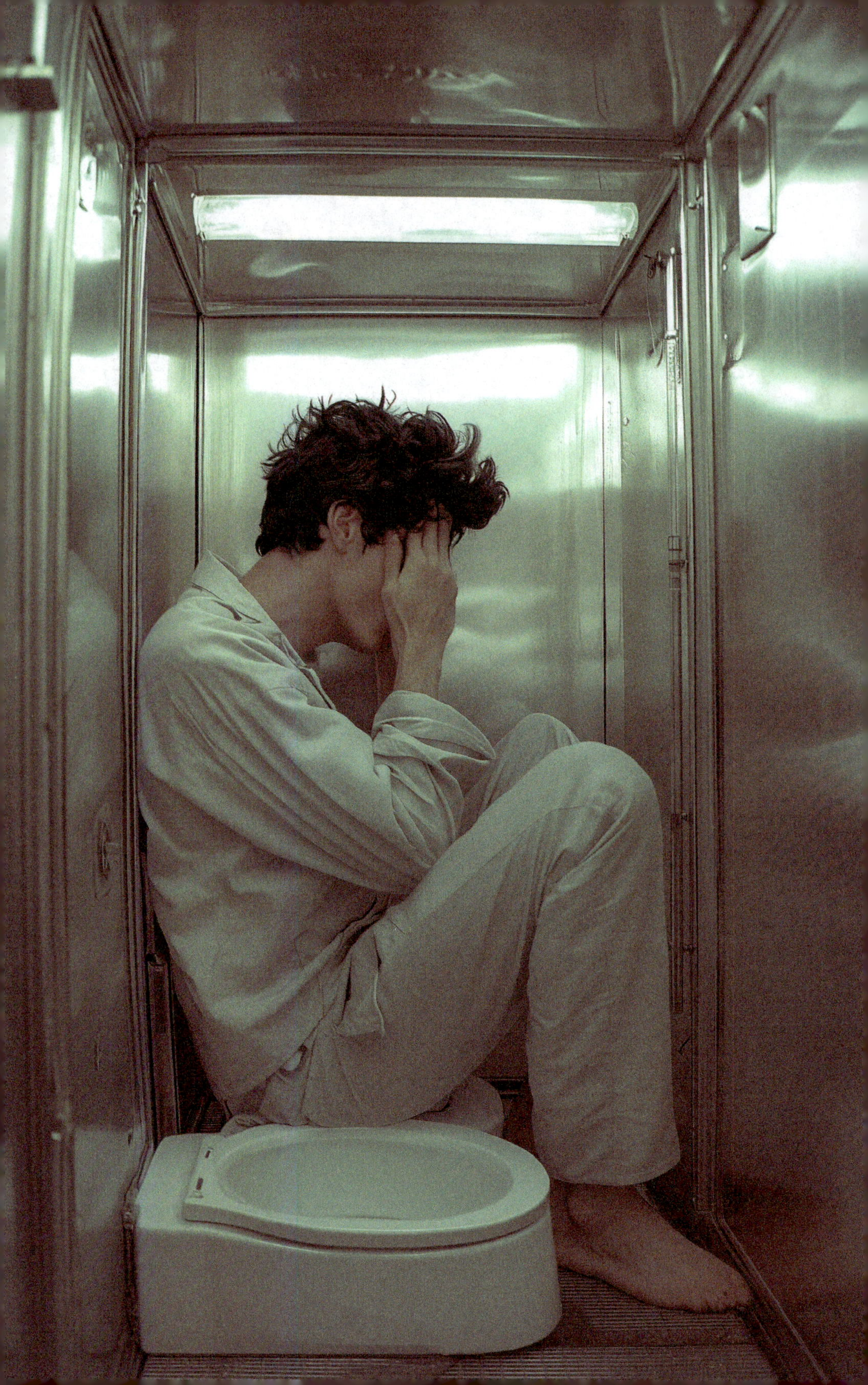

He meticulously examined every inch of the capsule, running his hands along the smooth walls, desperate for a crack or seam to pry open. But the walls were seamless and unforgiving. His shouts for help grew hoarse, fading into whispers swallowed by the empty space around him.

Just as he was on the verge of despair, after what felt like days, he heard something—a soft scrape followed by a dull thud. A thin slit opened at the base of the wall to his right, and a plate slid in. Pizza, lukewarm and dry, was offered up as if it were some cruel joke.

He barely noticed the wrinkled hand withdrawing into the shadows as he snatched the slice and devoured it. The food eased his hunger but brought to mind the metal toilet bolted in the corner, just inches away. He'd held off as long as he could, clinging to the hope of any other option.

Another meal arrived, and an idea sparked. He waited until the hand slid the pizza through and then lunged, gripping it tightly. The hand jerked back, struggling against his hold, but he refused to let go. He tugged, feeling the faint thud of his captor hitting the wall on the other side, then a final, heavy crash. Silence enveloped him. The hand was still.

For a moment, he expected to hear a shout, a curse—anything to shatter the oppressive silence—but nothing came. The fingers remained visible in the slit, stiff and unmoving. Days crept by in thick silence, each one marked only by his relentless hunger and the odor rising from the corner. He avoided looking at those fingers for as long as he could, but their im-

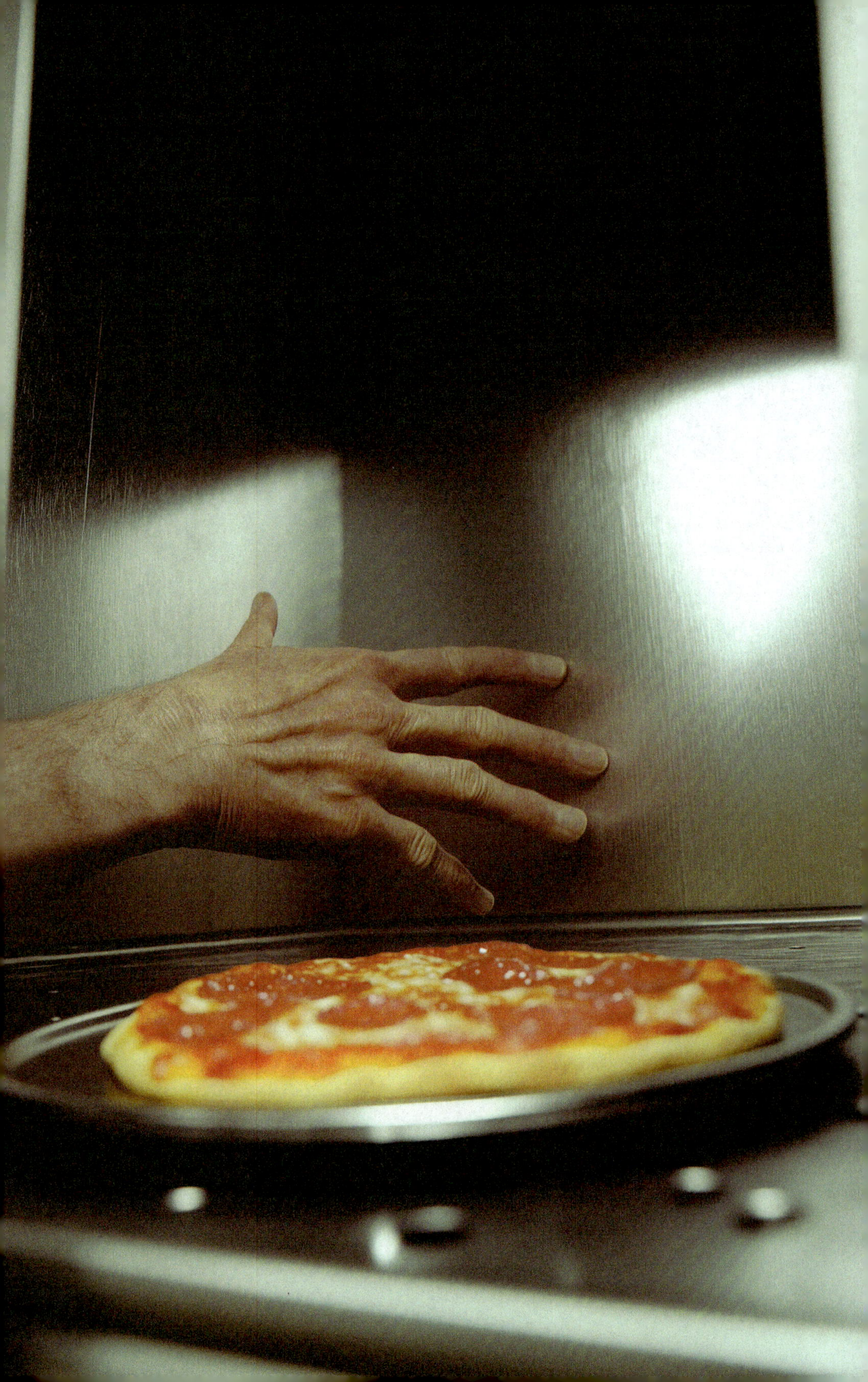

age crept back into his mind, a steady reminder of his desperate situation.

He thought about the toilet again. Maybe he could slip through it, force his way out somehow. The thought was both horrifying and liberating, a last resort that chilled him to the bone. In this dark confinement, the line between survival and despair blurred with every passing moment.

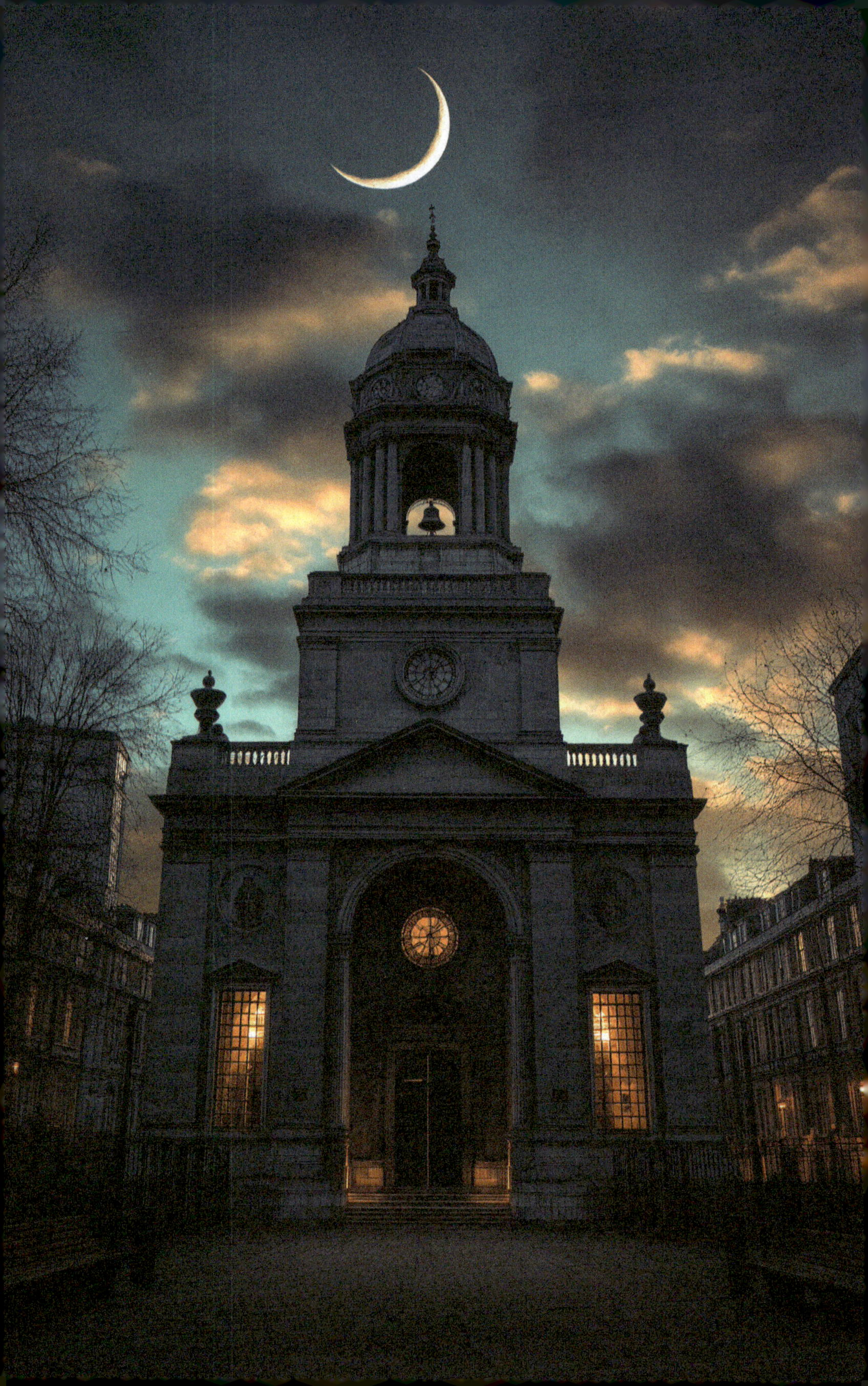

Secret Life

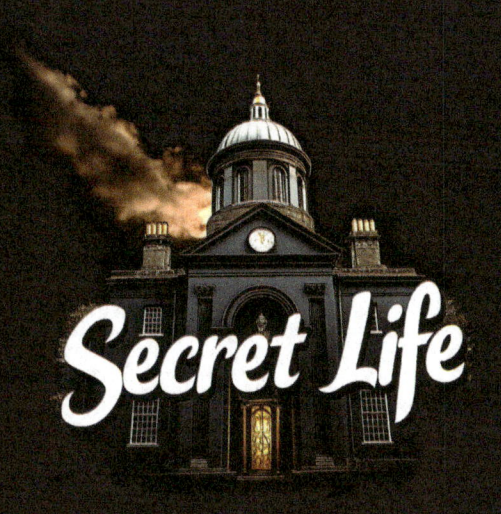

Cedric Langston had been a member of The Crimson Key for thirty-three years, a secret society whispered about in dark corners, known for its enigmatic rituals and relentless pursuit of truth. With an IQ of 160, Cedric had earned a reputation as a human lie detector, deciphering the subtle cues of deceit that danced in the shadows of men's faces. But beneath his façade of psychic prowess lay a troubling secret—he had developed a method to uncover lies not through any otherworldly gift, but through keen observation of body language and voice.

Today, three new initiates sat before him, blindfolded and masked, unaware of the gravity of the test ahead. Cedric watched intently as they answered the hundred questions he had meticulously crafted, each more complex than the last. The first candidate faltered at the sixth question, his voice trembling as he fabricated a story. The second managed to last until the ninth, his anxiety palpable. Then came Theodore, the third initiate, a figure cloaked in unsettling calm.

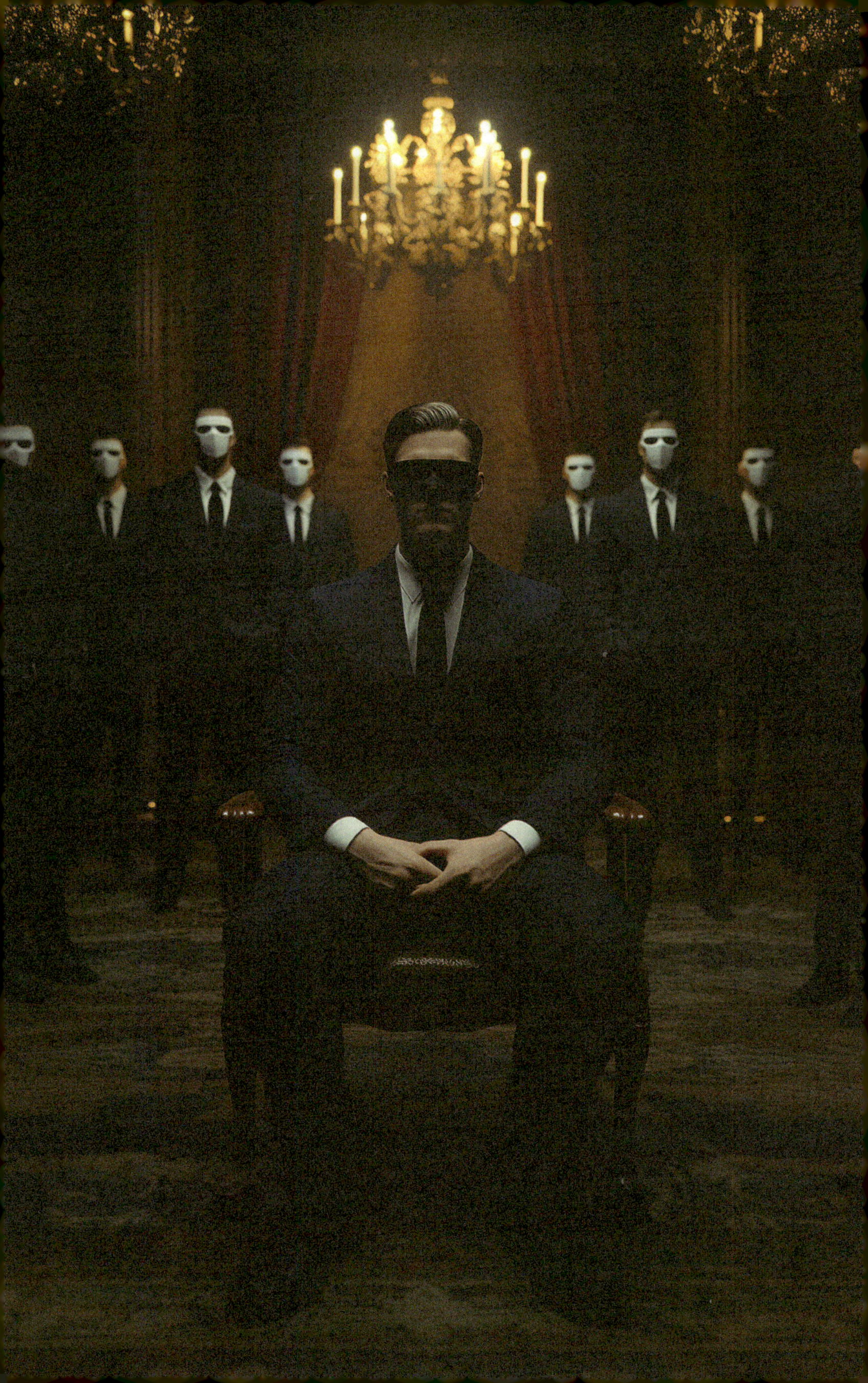

A shiver coursed through Cedric as Theodore took his seat. He answered every question with an eerie ease, his voice steady and betraying not a hint of discomfort. He spoke of train accidents, mysterious plane crashes, strange weather patterns, and the rise of artificial intelligence. Each answer flowed from him as if he were weaving a tapestry of truths, yet Cedric felt the air thicken with tension. How could he mask his body language so completely? Could it be that Theodore had somehow seen through the very process Cedric had devised? The uncertainty gnawed at him, a parasite burrowing into his thoughts.

Then came the final, bonus question, one that held the weight of the world in its simplicity: "Does God exist?"

The room fell into an almost suffocating silence, the atmosphere charged with electric fear. Cedric's pulse quickened, his palms dampening as he watched Theodore's face shift from serene confidence to something indescribable. The question hung in the air, grotesquely beautiful in its complexity. Theodore's eyes widened, revealing a glimpse of the storm within. For a moment, time itself seemed to twist around him.

And then, Theodore began to glow. A soft, unnatural light grew around him, intensifying into a white aura that enveloped his entire form. The brothers instinctively drew closer, transfixed, their breaths held as if bound by some invisible force. The light pulsed, blinding and beautiful, filling the room with an eerie stillness. Just as hands reached out to

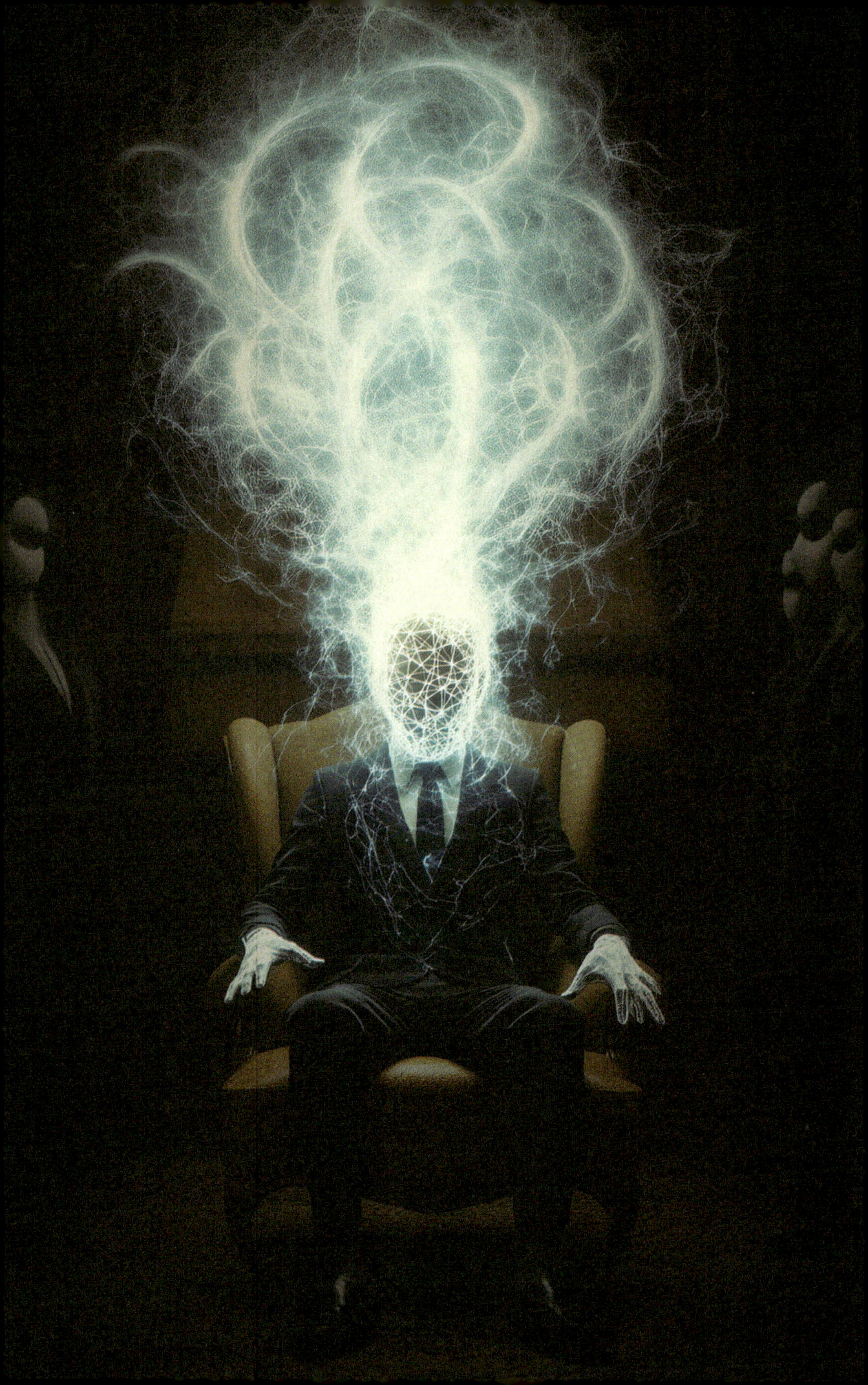

touch him, Theodore disappeared, vanishing into thin air as if he'd been a mirage.

A hushed gasp spread through the room. The initiates stood frozen, Cedric's heart pounding, the air thick with dread.

In the days following Theodore's disappearance, a heavy silence gripped The Crimson Key. Whispers of fear and speculation slithered through the dimly lit halls. The brothers pondered Theodore's final moments—had he glimpsed a truth so profound it transported him beyond their realm? Or had he been a pawn in a cosmic game, a god unaware of his own power?

Factions quickly emerged within the brotherhood, each convinced that Theodore's fate concealed terrible truths. The scientific lodge theorized he had breached a flaw in their reality itself, while the spiritual lodge whispered of divine ascension or punishment for seeking forbidden knowledge. An unsettling weight pressed down on them, a constant reminder that their quest for truth had led them into a dark and uncharted abyss.

The chilling legacy of that day loomed large, a dark cloud shadowing their every interaction. As the brothers convened in secret, haunted by Theodore's final question, they could no longer deny that they had crossed a threshold, one from which there might be no return.

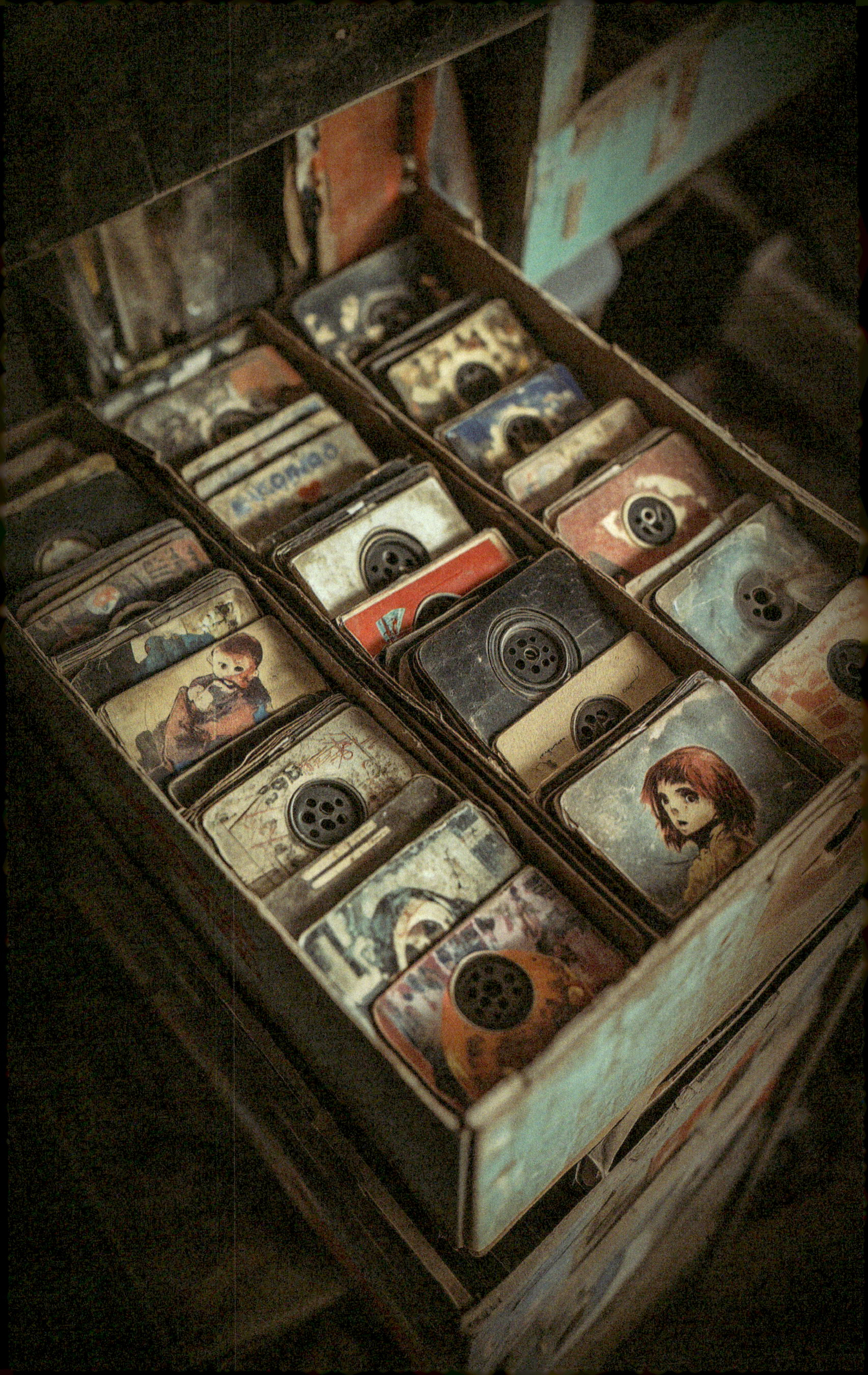

Final Episode

Leonard had just turned 74. His health had seen better days, compelling him to manage his anxieties, rest frequently, and maintain a strict diet. His children had moved to another state, leaving him feeling isolated and forgotten. In his quiet home, he often found himself reminiscing about the past, clinging to memories of simpler times.

One day, while sifting through the dusty corners of his attic, Leonard stumbled upon an old box filled with magnetic tapes. He recognized them immediately—these were the recordings of a childhood television show he adored in the 1960s. The tapes were marked with his childish drawings of the characters, but the name of the show was nowhere to be found.

Puzzled and nostalgic, Leonard felt a thrill of excitement mixed with unease. He remembered the joy the show had brought him, but he also sensed something unsettling lurking in the back of his mind.

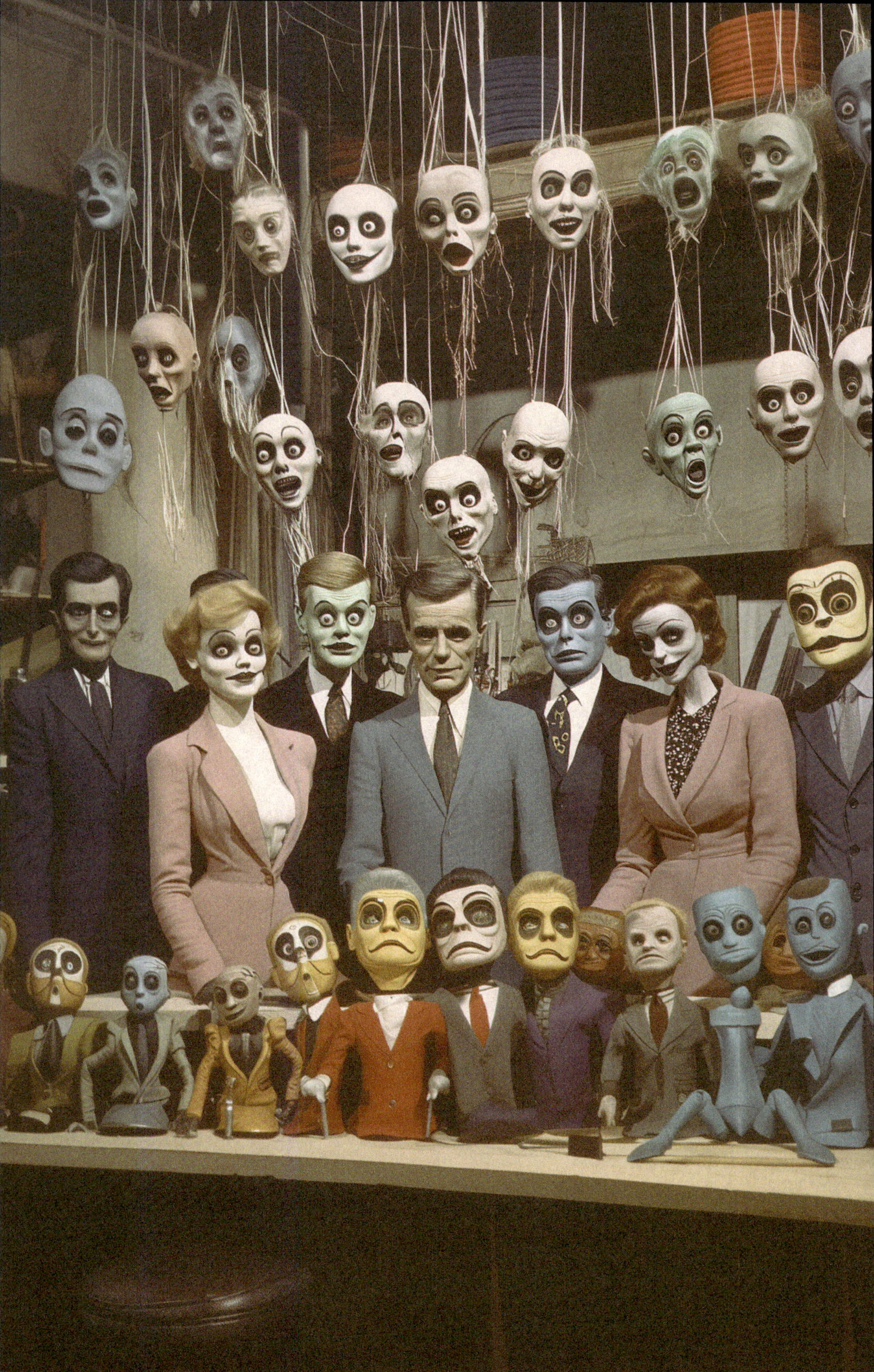

Eager to relive those moments, he searched for his old reel-to-reel tape player, scouring the attic until he finally found it buried beneath some boxes. His heart raced with anticipation as he set it up, but doubt gnawed at him. What if it didn't work? He hesitated, taking a moment to calm his racing heart before inserting the first tape. With a flick of the switch, he leaned back and watched.

As the screen flickered to life, Leonard felt an icy shiver run down his spine. The show was nothing like he remembered; it was far creepier, almost as if it had transformed into a horror movie overnight.

The host, a man named Abraham, stood center stage, flanked by six co-hosts, their puppet-like faces contorted in grotesque smiles. They stared directly at the screen, their eyes unsettlingly focused on Leonard, as though they were peering into his very soul.

Above them hung masks that appeared to twitch and respond to the events below, adding to the eerie atmosphere. The host presented a lineup of inanimate puppets on the desk, each one described in a voice that dripped with an unnatural enthusiasm. "These puppets," Abraham explained, "will grow to become real persons, just like us." Leonard's stomach churned at the implication, an unsettling feeling creeping over him.

Then, as if sensing Leonard's mounting dread, Abraham turned his gaze directly to him. "One of these puppets is you," he said, pointing to a small figure wearing a red shirt. Leon-

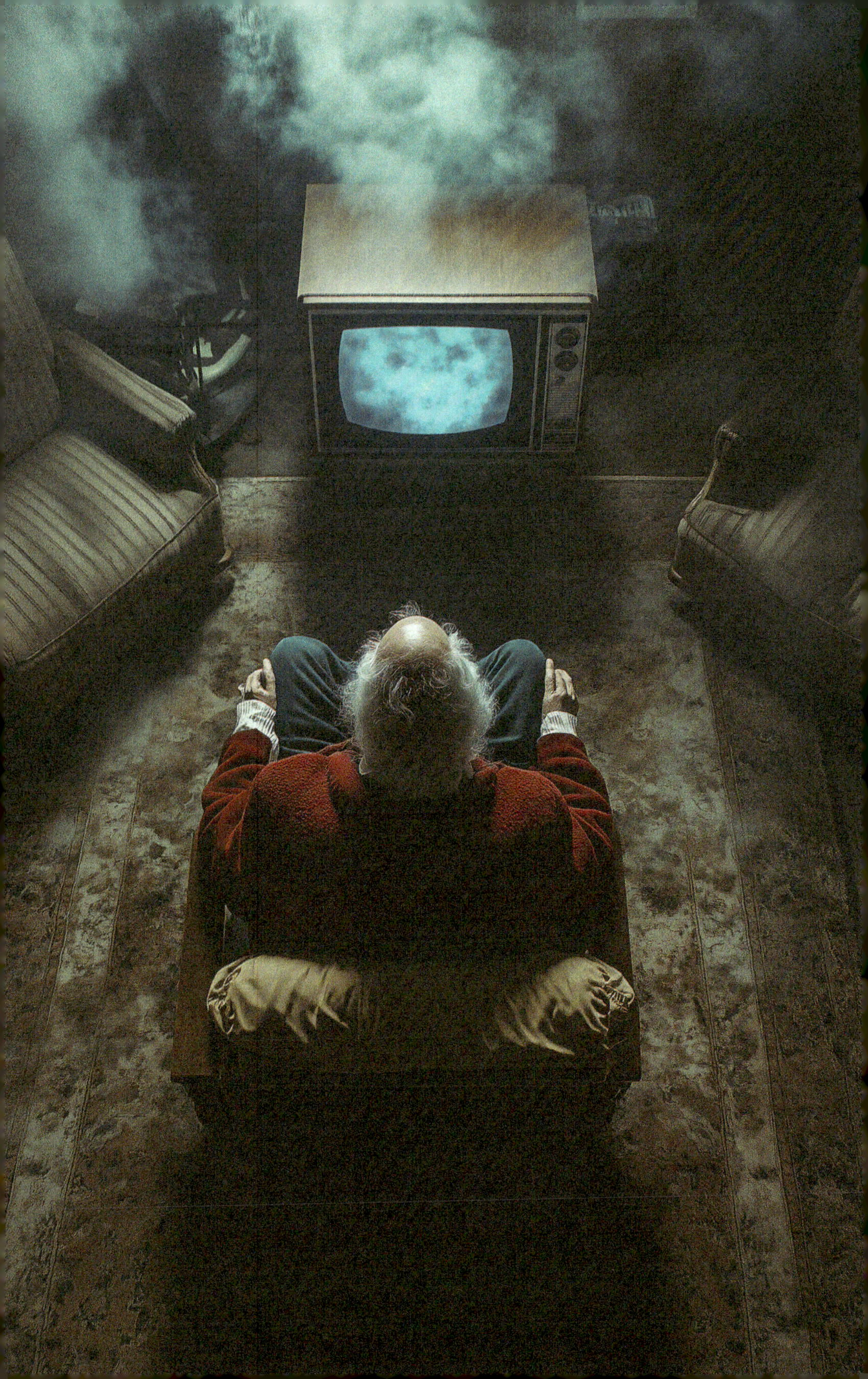

ard looked down at his own attire, the red fabric clinging to him like a shroud. A sickening realization dawned upon him as Abraham's voice echoed in his mind. "Let go, Leonard. We've all been dead a long time."

In an instant, Leonard felt his body growing light, as if the weight of his years was being stripped away. Panic surged through him as he watched in horror, his arms and legs stiffening, transforming into the rigid limbs of a puppet.

The world around him dissolved, replaced by the bright, surreal colors of the show. He could feel himself being pulled into the screen, his consciousness merging with the puppet dressed in the red shirt.

Now trapped behind glassy eyes, he looked out at the studio, a surreal audience filled with grinning faces watching him with delight. The laughter of the hosts became a thunderous applause, echoing in his ears, each roar twisting and warping like a malevolent choir.

Leonard, once a man full of memories, was now a puppet, forever entangled in a performance where he would never escape.